The Earl's Jilted Bride

Marriage by Obligation: Book 3

The Earl's Jilted Bride

Ruth Ann Nordin

This is a work of fiction. The events and characters described herein are imaginary and are not intended to refer to specific places or living persons. The opinions expressed in this manuscript are solely the opinions of the author and also represent the opinions or thoughts of the publisher.

The Earl's Jilted Bride
All Rights Reserved.
Copyright 2024 Ruth Ann Nordin
V1.0

Design Credit should state: Images and Cover Art Illustration by Period Images, Pi Creative Lab and MandyKoehlerDesigns43. Cover Text, Logo and Branding by Ruth Ann Nordin.

This book may not be reproduced, transmitted, or stored in whole or in part by any means including graphic, electronic, or mechanical without expressed written consent of the publisher/author except in the case of brief quotations embodied in critical articles and reviews.

If you love Regencies, here are more by Ruth Ann Nordin. (Listed in chronological order.) To see a complete list of Ruth's books, go to the end of this book.

<u>Marriage by Scandal Series</u>
The Earl's Inconvenient Wife
A Most Unsuitable Earl
His Reluctant Lady
The Earl's Scandalous Wife

<u>Marriage by Design Series</u>
Breaking the Rules
Nobody's Fool
A Deceptive Wager

<u>Standalone Regency</u>
Her Counterfeit Husband (happens during A Most Unsuitable Earl)

<u>Marriage by Deceit Series</u>
The Earl's Secret Bargain
Love Lessons With the Duke
Ruined by the Earl
The Earl's Stolen Bride

<u>Marriage by Arrangement Series</u>
His Wicked Lady
Her Devilish Marquess
The Earl's Wallflower Bride

Marriage by Bargain Series
The Viscount's Runaway Bride
The Rake's Vow
Taming The Viscountess
If It Takes A Scandal

Marriage by Fate Series
The Reclusive Earl
Married In Haste
Make Believe Bride
The Perfect Duke
Kidnapping the Viscount

Marriage by Fairytale Series
The Marriage Contract
One Enchanted Evening
The Wedding Pact
Fairest of Them All
The Duke's Secluded Bride

Marriage by Necessity Series
A Perilous Marriage
The Cursed Earl
Heiress of Misfortune

Marriage by Obligation Series
The Secret Admirer
Midnight Wedding
The Earl's Jilted Bride
Worth the Risk – coming soon
Anyone But You – coming soon

Chapter One

Author's Note: This book starts at the same time that Midnight Wedding (Book 2 in this series) does. There will be some overlap in the timelines.

March 1830

Reginald Bellington, the Duke of Havre, threw the door of the library open and stormed into the room. Lady Carol Bellington jerked, an action which resulted in her spilling tea on the book she'd been reading.

Reginald went over to her and shoved a missive in her face. "What's the meaning of this?"

Ignoring the book, she hurried to take the parchment before he snapped at her for being too slow. She placed the cup on the small table beside her and unfolded the missive. He, in turn, folded his arms and stared down at her in that intimidating way he had.

Her stomach twisted in dread. Without reading the thing, she already knew it was going to be horrible news. Though she'd been careful to do everything he wanted, she might have inadvertently upset someone.

It took her a moment to realize the missive wasn't from a reputable person in London reprimanding her for something she did. Instead, it was a…a…

She gasped. "This is a suicide note." Her gaze went to the author of the note. It was from the Duke of Augustine.

"Don't act surprised," Reginald growled. "He did it to get out of marrying you. I told you that you were being callous to him."

She opened her mouth to protest, but nothing came out. She hadn't liked the Duke of Augustine. Truth be told, she detested him. But to be fair, he had detested her. She didn't need the missive to explain that. She could always tell it by the way he glared at her whenever they were forced to be in the same room.

"You're to blame for this," Reginald continued as he paced the room. "All I could do as your uncle was fulfill your father's wishes. He's the one who arranged that marriage. Not me. But you told your silly friends I could get you out of the contract if I wanted to."

Her gaze left the missive so she could look at him. How dare he act like he couldn't do something? She wasn't a simpleton. She had read the contract herself, and it granted her guardian—father or otherwise—the right to dissolve the arrangement if it turned out it wasn't a compatible match. And the match most definitely hadn't been compatible. But if she pointed that out, then her uncle would know she had snuck into his bedchamber to read the contract.

Her uncle turned to her and put his hands on his hips. "Well, what are you going to do about this?"

Her eyes grew wide. What could she do? This was out of her control. She hadn't told the Duke of Augustine to kill himself. He'd done that all on his own, even though he'd made it abundantly clear in the missive he'd done it because he couldn't bear the thought of being married to her.

"You're useless," Reginald spat. "I blame your father for this. He pampered you. All of your life, he gave you everything you wanted, and he told you that you were intelligent and pretty and other nonsense that made you think more of yourself than you should." He let out a sigh and rolled his eyes. "You better hope someone marries you this Season because if someone doesn't, I'm sending you to a convent."

Her hand gripped the missive. While she wasn't all that excited about marriage, she did enjoy spending time with her friends. And he knew that. Which was why he'd made the threat.

Without another word, her uncle left the room. She let the missive fall to the floor and slumped back in her chair. It was like this every time he left. She could finally relax.

She hadn't realized how good her father had been to her until her uncle became her guardian. Growing up, she'd taken it for granted that the gentlemen in a lady's life sincerely cared about them. Her two dear friends, Rachel and Lydia, were fortunate that their brothers, who acted as their guardians, had their best interests at heart. She hoped they appreciated it.

She brushed a tear from her cheek. What was she supposed to do to get a gentleman to marry her? She didn't know the first thing about getting someone's attention. It was the ladies who knew how to flirt who had suitors lining up to visit them. She hadn't thought she'd need to develop those skills, so she hadn't bothered inquiring about them. That was an oversight she was quickly coming to regret.

Her gaze went to the book she'd been reading. The pages in front of her were now damp from the tea. She gently set the book, still open, on the table. Perhaps once the pages dried, the damage wouldn't be that terrible.

She stood up. She had more pressing matters to worry about than the condition of an old book. She had her future to consider. Who could help her? Rachel? Lydia? They were the only people she knew well enough to talk to about this. She retrieved the missive. She'd show them the letter and ask for their advice. If they didn't know what to do, maybe one of their brothers might help. Decision made, she left the townhouse.

***

"I shall miss Belladonna," Miss Amelia Carnel said.

Grant Carnel, the Earl of Wright, glanced at his sister as she came into the drawing room. Like her, he was going to miss their cousin. Belladonna had been good for Lucinda. With his sister entertaining suitors, he hadn't felt it right to ask her to watch his two-year-old daughter when he had to tend to his investments. But Belladonna was content to be single and had been delighted to take care of Lucinda. Unfortunately, her trip wasn't meant to last forever. She would have to return to Canada where her parents waited for her.

"I'm sure she'll be glad to return home," Grant told Amelia before he made sure Lucinda's bonnet was on correctly.

Lucinda grimaced and pushed her bonnet until it fell off of her head.

"You have to leave it alone, Lucinda," he said as he put the bonnet back on.

"Not like, Papa," Lucinda replied.

"You can't go outside without something on your head. You do want to see Belladonna get to the ship, don't you?"

Lucinda nodded in excitement and stopped fiddling with the bonnet. "Be good."

Grant smiled. Lucinda was so young that she spoke her mind. If only all people were like children. Then Grant would know whom he could trust and whom he couldn't.

"Why, don't you look pretty!" Belladonna called out as she came into the room. "Lucinda, you're going to be a beautiful lady someday. Gentlemen better watch their hearts when you're around."

Lucinda ran to Belladonna and hugged her legs. "Stay."

Belladonna smiled and gathered her into her arms. "I can't stay. I have too much to do back home. There are unfortunate children out there who don't have anyone to take care of them.

My job is to help raise them. Now," she continued as she set her back down, "I want to give you something to remember me by." She undid the strings of her reticule and pulled out a cameo. "I bought this for you when I was in the market." She pulled out a matching cameo. "I also bought one for myself. When I look at this, I'll think of you, and when you look at yours, you can think of me."

Grant felt a smile tug at his lips, but along with it came a sting of regret that Lucinda's mother hadn't had the warmth Belladonna and Amelia did. He forced back his tears so no one would notice. "I believe it's time to go. Thank you for coming to visit us, Belladonna. It was wonderful having you here."

"It really was," Amelia agreed. "Tell Uncle Josiah and Aunt Esther that we're glad they let you come to London."

"I will," Belladonna promised as she gave everyone a hug. "Thanks to you three, I have many good stories to tell the others when I get home. Amelia, you'll write me when you finally decide which of your suitors you've decided to marry, won't you?"

A blush crept up Amelia's cheeks. "When I decide, I will let you know."

Belladonna turned to Grant. "I wish you the best of luck in finding a wife. You can't let what happened at the Duke of Creighton's dinner party discourage you. There will be other ladies out there besides Miss Hamilton."

Grant resisted the urge to grimace. To his dying day, he wouldn't understand why Miss Lydia Hamilton had taken a fancy to Lord Quinton. He had offered to pay her a visit after the ill-fated dinner party since she had seemed like a pleasant lady. Unfortunately, she'd declined his offer, saying that she had decided to marry the other gentleman.

Amelia gave him a sympathetic smile. "The right lady is out there."

That was easy for someone who had gentlemen lining up to court her to say. He couldn't believe how easy it was for ladies to find someone. They didn't have to work at finding a husband. All they had to do was look attractive, and gentlemen lined up to talk to them.

"I better go so I'm not late," Belladonna said, drawing him back to the present.

"See ship, see ship!" Lucinda jumped up and down in excitement.

Amelia chuckled and picked Lucinda up. "There's no point in making the poor girl wait longer than she can bear."

Belladonna laughed, and Grant smiled so he wouldn't ruin the mood. He wanted Belladonna's last day here to be pleasant. He could dwell on his frustrations another time. He escorted everyone out of the townhouse. Sooner or later, he was bound to find a wife. Lucinda wasn't going to be without a mother forever. Maybe if he told himself this often enough, he'd start to believe it.

Chapter Two

Carol had never felt more alone in her entire life. She had written to Rachel and Lydia to tell them what had just happened. Then she asked them if she could visit them, only to find out they were both gone. Rachel—Rachel's brother had written back to her—had eloped to Gretna Green with the butler. Then the footman had sent word that Lydia and her brothers had left London to go to their country estate. Carol had no other friends she could confide in. She could understand one of them being gone, but why did both of them have to be gone at the same time?

Carol sat alone in her bedchamber. She was too scared to leave the safety of her room. Her uncle never bothered her when she was here. If she was anywhere else in the townhouse, he would likely hunt her down.

It was the most frustrating thing in the world to be born a lady. Her entire life was dictated by the gentlemen around her. She couldn't get her own townhouse, and thereby be relieved of living with her uncle. She had no female relatives to take her out, and the last thing she wanted to do was pretend to be happy while her uncle tried to shove her off to the first gentleman who happened to come along. Her only hope was that one of her friends might offer to let her live with them. But even then, who knew if her uncle would allow it?

A light knock came at her door. She frowned. She wasn't supposed to eat a meal this time of day, nor had her uncle set up a social engagement for her to attend. Why would the maid be knocking?

Maybe her uncle wanted her to start packing for the convent. While he'd only made the threat three days ago, he was also horribly impatient. He might not allow her the rest of the Season to find a husband.

She reluctantly stood up and went to the door. She opened it a crack and peered behind her lady's maid to make sure she was alone. She relaxed when she didn't see her uncle, but only slightly. "What is it?" Carol asked.

"His Grace wishes to see you in the drawing room," the maid replied. "I am to tell you to put on a pretty gown and fix your hair first. Would you like my assistance with that?"

Her stomach tensed. What was Reginald planning? He wasn't the spontaneous type. He didn't like going to a social event unless he had it planned out well in advance. With an uncertain breath, Carol opened the door farther and gestured for the maid to come into the room. It must be important if her uncle had involved her lady's maid. Carol had relieved her of her duties for the afternoon since she didn't think she was going to need her for anything.

This particular maid was young, probably thirteen or fourteen. Though she didn't know much about styling hair, Carol didn't trust her shaky hands to do a good job. She'd been on pins and needles since finding out the Duke of Augustine hung himself. Yes, she would be spared a marriage to him, but the inquiries her uncle had been making about convents let her know just how serious he was about getting rid of her.

Her uncle had purchased several black gowns for her to wear. She put one on, even though it seemed to mock what her relationship to the duke had been. He hadn't loved her, nor had she loved him. In truth, they detested each other. But her uncle was determined to make it appear as if his death caused both him and her a deep sorrow. And with her uncle, appearances were everything.

The maid, as it turned out, did a fine job with her hair. Carol was so surprised she even commented on it. The maid seemed pleased by the compliment before she hurried to leave the room.

Carol braced herself for whatever occasion her uncle had in mind. She just prayed it wasn't a trip to the priest's so he could find out more about convents. Or worse, she hoped he wouldn't throw her on a carriage so she could live in one. No. He wouldn't throw her out of here without having her clothes packed first, would he?

When Carol made it to the drawing room, she saw an unfamiliar gentleman, who looked to be in his early thirties, talking to her uncle. Her uncle seemed unusually happy with the visit. Was it possible he was a clergyman from another parish?

Upon noticing her, the two gentlemen stood, but it was her uncle who hurried over to her. "This is Lady Carol, my dutiful niece. Carol, my dear, this is Lord Wright."

Lord Wright? She tried to place the title. She'd heard it before, but for the life of her, she couldn't remember where. At least, the gentleman wasn't a vicar or priest who was here to discuss life as a nun with her. She offered him a polite greeting, which he returned, then sat in the chair her uncle gestured to.

"I can't tell you how heartbroken she was when news came of her betrothed's untimely parting from this world," her uncle said as he handed her a cup of tea. "Of course, I'm also upset by the situation. It was such a shock. No one knew the Duke of Augustine didn't want to live."

She didn't know what to say. If her uncle wanted her to play the part of the sad lady, she couldn't follow along with it. She settled for taking a sip of her tea.

"Death is never pleasant, no matter what the circumstances are," Lord Wright commented. "I hope the pain isn't too great."

Noting that he directed the last statement to her, she glanced his way. She was struck by the tenderness in his expression. Besides her friend's brothers, she couldn't recall the last time a gentleman looked upon her favorably. Except, Lord Wright had something else in his expression that she didn't recognize. She took a closer look at him. He was attractive. Dark hair, bright green eyes, full lips. She'd never felt a stirring of attraction for any of the gentlemen she'd come across, but she did with him.

As soon as the thought came to her, she shoved it aside. She was certain that, whoever this gentleman was, he was already married. Therefore, she had no right to think of him in such a way.

"Death is never pleasant," her uncle spoke in a thoughtful manner. "And it's even worse when the person is so young. The Duke of Augustine was like a son to me. I was looking forward to making him a part of the family." With a regretful shrug, he drank his tea.

Carol couldn't believe what she was hearing. Her uncle might have gotten along with His Grace well enough, but in no way did he think of him as a son. Resisting the urge to point this out, she took another sip of her tea.

"My dear," her uncle began in a sweet voice that let her know he expected her to be obedient in what he wanted, "Lord Wright is acquainted with the Duke of Creighton. Isn't the Duke of Creighton your friend's brother? What is the name of that friend?"

Not sure where he was going with this, she answered, "Lady Rachel."

Her uncle nodded. "That's the one. Lady Rachel is lovely. She comes from a reputable family, too. I think if the Duke of Creighton were to recommend someone for you to marry, that recommendation is worth noting."

"I don't mind making the proposal myself," Lord Wright spoke up.

She turned her attention back to Lord Wright. He wasn't already married? He was here to discuss marrying her?

Lord Wright placed the cup on the table and shifted in the chair. "I met the Duke of Creighton two months ago. At his dinner party, I met Lady Rachel. As your uncle said, she is a lovely lady, but I could tell she was interested in another gentleman who happened to be in attendance at that dinner party." He paused. "I'll be upfront with you, Lady Carol. I am a widower of a two-year-old girl who needs a mother. I've been searching for a lady who is willing to take on that role. The Duke of Creighton sent me word about your situation. He said that you have a kind and giving heart. Based on that, I asked your uncle if I might pay you a visit and see if you'd be willing to marry me."

Carol dropped her cup. Her uncle reached out and grabbed it before it fell on the floor. Thankfully, there was so little tea in it that she didn't make a mess.

She couldn't believe it. She needed a husband, and she'd had no idea where she was going to find one. Now, out of nowhere, Lord Wright came to save her from being dragged off to a convent. She'd be a fool to turn down the offer, especially when she didn't get that horrible sensation of doom with Lord Wright that she'd gotten around the Duke of Augustine.

"I will marry you," she hurried to reply.

Lord Wright didn't hide his surprise. He hadn't expected her to say yes, at least not right away. But she saw no reason to delay the answer.

Her uncle laughed and set her cup on the table. "I told you she's always wanted to be a mother. I knew that as soon as she heard about the little girl she couldn't say no."

He knew no such thing, but she kept the comment to herself. Her uncle was just as eager to get her out of there as she was to leave. Lord Wright was offering both of them that opportunity.

"Wonderful," Lord Wright said after he overcame his shock. "I'll arrange for a special license so we can marry." He glanced at her uncle. "Given the situation with the Duke of Augustine, it might be best to make the marriage a private affair. Undoubtedly, people are talking about the way he died."

Reginald nodded. "You make a good point. There's no sense in encouraging more gossip. We'll go with a special license."

Grant turned his gaze to her. "Is that all right with you?"

"I'm fine with having a quick wedding," she assured him. "We don't even need to go through the formality of a wedding breakfast. To be honest, I don't like large gatherings."

It was true. She didn't like large gatherings. She felt most comfortable with her friends. The only reason she hadn't panicked at the balls was because she didn't have to worry about attracting a suitor. It left her free to talk with her friends.

"All right," Lord Wright agreed. "As I said, I'll arrange for a special license. I would like for you to meet my daughter before we marry. She's only two. I don't know how much she'll understand about what's going on, but I'd like for her to know you'll be her mother before we exchange vows. I think it'll make things easier for her."

Carol nodded. "That sounds sensible. I'd be happy to meet her."

"I'll introduce you to her at my dinner party," Lord Wright said. "When will be a good evening for me to host it?"

"Lady Carol has no pressing engagements on her social calendar," her uncle answered for her. "You can host it at your earliest convenience."

She joined the two gentlemen as they rose to their feet. Her uncle mentioned how glad he was that Carol wouldn't have to endure the burden of spinsterhood as he saw Lord Wright to the door. Lord Wright glanced back at her, as if he had wished she was the one leading him out instead of her uncle. She didn't know how to respond to that. The Duke of Augustine never looked back to see her when he was leaving.

Once the two gentlemen were out of the room, she decided to hurry back to her bedchamber so she wouldn't have to face her uncle until dinner.

Chapter Three

"She said yes? Right away? Without taking any time to think over your proposal?" Amelia asked Grant later that day as they took a stroll through Hyde Park.

Lucinda stopped to study something in the grass nearby, so they stopped, too.

Grant turned to face his sister. "Do you think something is wrong with her?"

Amelia paused for a moment. "Well, no. It doesn't mean something is wrong with her. It's just that if a stranger came to visit me and offered marriage, I'd have to take some time to think it over."

"Maybe she likes the idea of being a mother. Her uncle did mention how much she wants a child."

"I want a child, too, but I also want to know the gentleman I'll be marrying. Marriage is for life. Why wouldn't she want to find out if you're going to be a good husband?"

"Perhaps it's because she trusts the Duke of Creighton's judgment. I trust his judgment. He thinks she'll be a good match for me. He said Lady Carol is kind and considerate and that she cares about people."

She arched an eyebrow. "If she's so wonderful, then why doesn't he marry her?"

"He thinks of her as another sister."

"He wrote that?"

"Yes, he did." Grant paused then added, "Lady Carol is good friends with his sister. We met his sister at his dinner party. You like Lady Rachel."

Amelia considered his argument and nodded. "You're right. I do like her. She thought Lord Quinton was as strange as you, Belladonna, and I did. That proves she has good sense."

"Her brother shows good sense, too." He glanced at Lucinda to make sure she was still nearby before saying, "Her brother apologized for inviting Lord Quinton to the dinner party. He said if he had known Lord Quinton was going to insist on exchanging partners, he never would have asked him to come over. Lord Quinton ruined things for all of us."

"That's not true for all of us. Mr. St. George ended up being my escort, and I think he wants to be my suitor."

"What about Lord Compton and Mr. Everson? I thought you liked them."

"Yes, I suppose they're all right."

"You're a lady, and as a lady, you have your pick of gentlemen to choose from. I advise you to take your time in selecting the best one."

"I am taking my time." She gave him a pointed look. "This is why I can't believe Lady Carol accepted your proposal right away. You'd think she would take her time, too."

He was sure she would if she hadn't just learned her betrothed hung himself. He didn't know the details of the gentleman's death, but the whole thing was marked with scandal. All of London was talking about it. He suspected she was eager to marry because her prospects had suddenly diminished. Not many gentlemen wanted to court a lady whose betrothed committed suicide.

"Well," Amelia began, "if Lady Carol is a friend of Lady Rachel's, then she must be nice. Miss Lydia Hamilton is Lady Rachel's friend, and she's nice." She chuckled. "She might be strange for liking Lord Quinton, but she is nice."

Grant shook his head. He didn't like the reminder that Lord Quinton appealed to Miss Hamilton more than he did. He didn't consider himself to be a vain gentleman, but his pride had been pricked by that situation. He'd like to think he was a better prospect for marriage than Lord Quinton. At least he didn't make it a habit of complaining about every little thing around him.

"I hope this marriage will go better for you than your first one did," Amelia said in a soft voice.

Grant met his sister's gaze and noted the sympathy there. He hadn't given her any details of his marriage to Fiona. He had only said that it was a shame Lucinda didn't have a mother, though, as he thought on it, Fiona hadn't even cared that she'd had a child. That wasn't surprising, Grant supposed, since she hadn't cared that she'd had a husband.

"Papa, Auntie Ama," Lucinda called out.

Amelia smiled at her attempt to say her full name, and at once, Grant felt his mood lighten.

Lucinda came over to them with a caterpillar in her hand.

"Be careful with that," Amelia said as she loosened the girl's grip on the insect. "It's a small creature. You don't want to squash it."

The caterpillar walked across her hand, and Lucinda laughed. "Feels funny."

"I'm sure it does." Amelia helped the girl hold the caterpillar so it didn't fall to the ground.

Grant noticed Mr. St. George approaching, so he took the caterpillar from them and set it on the ground. When Lucinda protested, he whispered, "You need to let the thing go. We can't take it home with us." He took Lucinda by the hand. "There's someone who looks like he wants to talk to your aunt." He hadn't told Amelia, but Mr. St. George had expressed an interest in being her suitor.

When Amelia noticed Mr. St. George, a blush crept up her cheeks. She fiddled with the curls poking out from under her hat. Grant blinked in surprise. Yes, she had just told him she fancied Mr. St. George, but Grant hadn't realized just how much she fancied him. Her face glowed with the anticipation of talking to him. It was a shame no lady had ever looked at him that way.

"Good afternoon, Mr. St. George," Grant greeted. "How is your day going?"

"It's going well." Mr. St. George's gaze went to Amelia, and his smile widened. "I just took a stroll through the market. I saw the ad you mentioned in the newspaper from someone who is trying to sell his wife."

Amelia gasped. "You didn't believe me when I told you there was such an ad?"

He shrugged. "You have to admit it's absurd that someone would sell his wife. I didn't think such a thing was legal."

"It's rarely ever done, but there are such ads from time to time, and it's usually from someone not from nobility," Grant inserted.

"That explains why the newspaper was in a discreet place," Mr. St. George said. "I doubt many from the Ton would see it."

"Did you go to Sir Elton's shop to find it?" Amelia asked.

He nodded. "And that shop has a lot of odd things in it like you said."

"I'm a bit insulted you didn't take my word for it. I'd like to think you would trust me."

Though Amelia offered a pout, Grant caught the flirtatious spark in her eyes.

Mr. St. George put his hand over his heart. "I promise to never doubt you again."

"Make sure you don't," she replied.

After a moment, he asked, "What is your favorite oddity Sir Elton sells?"

She paused for a moment as her gaze went upward to the right. "It's not my favorite, but it's what I think of first when someone mentions his store. That is the shrunken human head. Sir Elton claims it's real, but I hope it's not. Can you imagine having something like that in your home?" She shuddered.

"I didn't see that anywhere in the shop."

"Maybe he had to get rid of it. It was a monstrosity."

"Or he could have sold it," Grant inserted.

"Who would want such a thing?" she asked in shock.

Grant shrugged. "There are some strange people out there."

"The strangest thing I saw in his shop was the tie pin made from someone's tooth," Mr. St. George said. "Sir Elton swore the tooth belonged to King George III. I didn't purchase it. I did purchase the tie pin made from a ruby, though." He reached into the pocket of his waistcoat and showed it to them.

"Toy, toy," Lucinda said and raised her hand toward it.

"No, that's not a toy," Grant replied and urged her to put her arm down. He picked her up so she wouldn't run over to Mr. St. George. "That's a gentleman's tie pin. He's going to wear it. Being a girl, you have your pretty cameo."

Lucinda pointed to her new cameo and told Mt. St. George, "From Bella."

Amelia turned to Mr. St. George. "Belladonna is on her way back to Canada. She gave my niece that as a gift to remember her by."

"That's a nice gesture," Mr. St. George replied. "I'm sorry I wasn't able to say goodbye to her before she left."

"We would have enjoyed your visit." Amelia gave Grant a hopeful look.

Picking up on the hint, Grant spoke up. "I've recently become engaged, and I thought I'd have a dinner party to introduce the lady to my family. Why don't you come so that my sister has someone to escort her?"

"I'd be delighted to attend," he replied. "In fact," his gaze went to Amelia, "I have something I wish to speak to you about. The dinner party would be the ideal time to do that."

Noting the excitement on his sister's face, Grant promised him, "I'll send you an invite after I find out when my future bride is able to attend."

"I'll keep my schedule clear," Mr. St. George said before he wished them a good day and headed down the path.

Lucinda wiggled in Grant's arms. "Down, down."

He set her down, and the girl started off down the path. Since her little legs made her slow, he and Amelia quickly caught up to her.

"What does Mr. St. George want to talk to me about?" Amelia asked in a low voice.

He took a good look at the excited expression on her face and shook his head. "This is for him to say, not me."

"Oh, don't be like that. You can give me a hint."

He laughed. "No. I'm not going to ruin this for him. You'll just have to wait."

When she groaned, he laughed harder. His sister would be thrilled when Mr. St. George asked to be her suitor, and there was no way he was going to spoil that for Mr. St. George. The gentleman had a right to see how much this excited her. Every gentleman should be lucky enough to know the lady he wished to be with wanted to be with him, too.

Chapter Four

No matter how much her uncle protested, Carol couldn't stop fidgeting as the carriage took her to Lord Wright's townhouse. Next to her, her uncle let out a frustrated sigh. She made another attempt to stay still, but it was no use.

"I'm glad that I only have to drop you off at his townhouse and pick you up when it's time to take you home," he muttered. "If I had to put up with this all evening, I'd throw myself off the top of the roof."

"I'm sorry," she forced out in an attempt to appease him.

She wished the wedding was already over, but it wasn't due for another two days. One would think her uncle would be satisfied with that. She was almost out of his residence. But each day passed by slower than the one before.

I hope you're more pleasant to Lord Wright than you were to the Duke of Augustine," her uncle said.

She had been as pleasant as she could possibly be to the Duke of Augustine. He rarely ever talked to her, but when he did, he kept his words curt. Even now, she inwardly shivered when thinking of him. At times, it still felt like he was hovering nearby with that scowl. She pulled the shawl closer around her shoulders.

Mercifully, her uncle remained silent the rest of the way to the townhouse, and he only stayed long enough to ask Lord Wright when he should return for Carol. Even if Carol was attending a dinner party with unfamiliar people, it was better than being with him.

"I'm glad you could make it," Lord Wright told her as her uncle left. "Lucinda will be going up with the nursemaid before we eat, but I wanted you to meet her. I also wanted her to meet you since you'll be her mother."

She didn't know if it was his smile or the gentle tone in his voice, but the knot in her stomach eased. Feeling shy, she returned his smile. "How old did you say she was?"

"She's two. She doesn't remember her mother." In a lower voice, he added, "My late wife died about a month after giving birth to her."

"I'm sorry," Carol replied. "That must have been a terrible shock."

"It couldn't be more terrible than the shock you went through with your betrothed."

Yes, it had been a shock. Truth be told, it still was. But it was a relief, too. She didn't want to say this, lest he think she was an awful person. Who else would be glad to see someone die?

"I'll escort you to the drawing room," he offered as he extended his arm.

Pushing aside her morbid thoughts, she accepted his arm and walked down the hall with him.

Her gaze went to a young lady who was dancing with a little girl. Rachel had told her Lord Wright's sister was Miss Carnel. This lady had to be her.

Miss Carnel stopped dancing as soon as she noticed them. "Forgive us. I had to distract Lucinda so she wouldn't run to see who was at the door."

"Bella!" Lucinda called out and peered around Carol.

Though Carol knew no one had followed them into the room, she glanced behind her.

"Belladonna is our cousin," Lord Wright explained. "And she returned to Canada a few days ago. Lucinda misses her."

"It's a shame you didn't get a chance to meet her," Miss Carnel said. "You would have liked her."

Since Carol didn't know what else to say, she replied, "I'm sure I would have."

"Lucinda," Lord Wright began, "this is the lady I'll be marrying. She's going to be your new mother."

The way he said that made her role in the marriage seem so important. She didn't know anything about children. She hoped she was up to the task. Forcing aside her uncertainty, she offered the girl a smile and greeted her.

The girl gave a greeting in return then showed her the cameo she was wearing. "From Bella."

Miss Carnel laughed. "She won't stop talking about this thing. She points it out to everyone who comes by. Belladonna gave that to her before she left."

"What a lovely gesture," Carol said.

"Yes, it was. We all miss having her here, but we're happy to welcome you to the family," Miss Carnel replied. "Come and sit. Make yourself at home."

When Lord Wright nodded his approval, Carol went over to the seats. After a moment, she chose the settee, thinking that since she was engaged to Lord Wright, he would sit next to her. Thankfully, when he settled beside her, she didn't feel a blast of coldness coming from him that she'd felt whenever she was forced to sit near the Duke of Augustine. That made her relax even more. Perhaps this marriage might work in her favor.

Lord Wright brought Lucinda onto his lap. "I suppose we can dismiss the formalities since we are to be married. I am Grant, and my sister is Amelia."

"I'm Carol." Recalling they must have already realized that because she was formally known as *Lady Carol*, her cheeks warmed. When it came to social functions, her friends made it seem so easy to converse with other people. What was their secret?

Amelia sat in a nearby chair. "Carol is a pretty name. It makes me think of joy and happiness. Kind of like the carols we sing at Christmastime. Those always lift my spirits."

Carol had never thought of her name that way before, but since Amelia was extending the compliment, she thanked the lady.

"Lucinda likes to sing," Amelia continued after a moment of silence passed between everyone. "She doesn't sing all of the words, of course, but she can hum along with a tune, and she will sing a couple of words."

"She even makes some words up," Grant inserted. "Though, to be fair, some of the lyrics are difficult to remember."

"I think she'll have a lovely singing voice when she's older," Amelia said. "She does a much better job holding a tune than I do. Can you hold a tune, Carol?"

Carol shook her head. "I stopped singing when my father thought I was in pain."

The two laughed, and Carol was relieved her answer had been considered witty. It wasn't like her to be witty. Usually, Lydia was the witty one.

"Pretty hair," Lucinda said.

Surprised, Carol turned her attention to the girl. "Pardon?"

"Hair." Lucinda pointed to her hair, which was pulled up with pins. "Pretty."

Without thinking, Carol touched her hair. "Oh, thank you."

"She's right," Grant began. "You do have pretty hair."

"The curls are nice," Amelia agreed. "I have a doll from childhood with hair like yours."

"Get doll?" Lucinda asked.

"Not now," Grant gently told her. "Amelia can show her the doll after she comes to live here."

For a moment, Carol recalled how nice her own father had been with her. Her heart warmed at the memory. Living with her uncle, she had a tendency to forget how good her father had been to her. Surely, he would have released her from the marriage to the Duke of Augustine if he'd been alive to do so. Her father had died when she was twelve. That had been before she'd even met the Duke of Augustine.

What a strong contrast this dinner party was turning out to be compared to the ones Carol had been forced to attend at the Duke of Augustine's townhouse. To get through those, she'd actually snuck in some sherry to help settle her nerves. It was a secret she'd never told anyone, not even her friends, and usually, she told her friends everything. But how could they understand just how awful that betrothal had been? Unless one went through something like that, they couldn't truly comprehend it.

"Mr. St. George has arrived," the butler called out.

Carol's attention went to the other guest who was to attend the dinner party tonight. She recognized the name. Rachel had been sure he'd been her secret admirer but later admitted to being wrong.

Grant took a moment to make the introductions, and Amelia gave Mr. St. George a cup of tea and gestured for him to sit and make himself comfortable.

"We're glad you could make it this evening," Grant told Mr. St. George. "Lucinda will be going to bed soon. I just wanted to introduce her to the lady I'll be marrying."

"I don't mind that the child is here," Mr. St. George assured them. "I was a child once. I remember how fun it was to be with the adults."

"I don't know," Amelia said. "All I remember is being bored when our parents would sit and talk with their friends. I hope we're not boring you, Lucinda."

Lucinda shook her head. "Stay up."

Mr. St. George chuckled. "The best part about being with the adults is that you get to stay up a little bit later. Sleep is boring when you're a child."

"It's not boring when you're an adult," Grant countered. "Sometimes I look forward to going to bed after a long day."

Mr. St. George shook his head. "Not me. I spent my entire life in the country. I want to be awake to take in as much of London as I can."

Lucinda yawned, and Grant smiled. "Well, unlike you, a little girl can't stay up for long. She needs her rest." He glanced at his sister. "Do you mind if I leave you and Mr. St. George for a moment? I need to summon the maid, but I also want to speak with Carol for a moment."

Carol hid her apprehension. Just when she was beginning to feel like everything was going to be all right, she was being summoned to speak with Grant alone. He wasn't going to tell her he had changed his mind about the marriage, was he?

Carol forced herself to get up and follow Grant to the side of the room. From the other side of the room, Mr. St. George and Amelia spoke in low tones.

Grant pulled a cord on the wall then told Carol, "I thought I'd keep the first meeting between you and Lucinda brief. I was able to finish my business dealings so I am free for tomorrow. Would you be interested in me bringing Lucinda over to your townhouse tomorrow? We can go out to Hyde Park or check out the animals at the menagerie or some other activity you enjoy."

Carol breathed a sigh of relief. Things were still going well this evening.

"Animals, animals," Lucinda said.

"It's not polite to interrupt," Grant kindly admonished her. "Lady Carol needs to answer first."

Carol had thought seeing the animals sounded like fun, but even if she had preferred another activity, the girl's hopeful expression would have convinced her to do what she wanted. "I think the menagerie sounds like fun."

Carol was rewarded with a wide smile from the child, and she was glad she'd been able to make her happy.

"We'll go to the menagerie then," Grant said. "Will your uncle be able to chaperone, or should I bring my sister with us?"

So as not to let him know how horrified she'd be to have her uncle come along, she counted to three before she spoke. "I like your sister," she managed to calmly say. "I'd like it if she came with us."

Grant smiled. "Amelia will join us then."

The maid arrived, and Carol wished the girl a good night's sleep before the maid whisked her away. Before returning to the others, Grant whispered to Carol, "Thank you for showing an interest in Lucinda."

Carol thought that was an odd thing for him to say, but he put his hand under her elbow and escorted her to the settee before she could ask about it.

Chapter Five

"Reuben asked to be my suitor," Amelia confided to Carol after she and Carol settled into the drawing room after dinner. "I was hoping he would, but I wasn't sure. I don't see him as much as I see Lord Compton. Lord Compton has been coming by twice a week to visit. Even Mr. Everson has been here a couple of times. I barely see Reuben."

"Reuben's very interested in you," Carol said as she held the teacup in her hands. "He barely took his eyes off of you during dinner.

A blush crept up Amelia's face. "Can I share something that will be just between the two of us?"

"I'm good at keeping secrets."

Amelia leaned in closer to her and whispered, "I like Reuben more than Lord Compton and Mr. Everson. I'm hoping now that he's asked to be my suitor, a proposal won't be far away."

Carol studied the lady's face and envied her. It must be wonderful to be in love. Amelia practically glowed, and her eyes sparkled. The only other times she'd seen someone look like that was when Rachel spoke of her secret admirer and Lydia spoke of Lord Quinton.

"My brother is looking forward to being married to you," Amelia said after a long moment passed between them.

Surprised, Carol turned her gaze back to her. "He is?"

"He was beginning to give up hope on finding someone to marry. He's talked to so many gentlemen about their sisters, daughters, and cousins. Ever since his return to London, all he's done is look for a wife so Lucinda can have a mother."

Oh, so that was why he was looking forward to the marriage. Though disappointed, Carol couldn't be surprised. He had come out and told her he wanted a mother for the little girl.

Amelia giggled. "You're friends with Lady Rachel. Did she tell you about that dinner party her brother hosted where she met me and Grant?"

"She said the evening turned out to be a disaster."

"The dinner certainly wasn't what any of us expected. Lord Quinton was supposed to be my escort, but he didn't like the green and blue cameo I was wearing. He said it was bad luck."

"How could it be bad luck?"

Amelia shrugged. "That one still baffles me. All I know is that he claimed it was in the image of a peacock eye, but I know for a fact that the person who made it had no such thing in mind when he created it. We tried to reason with him, but he insisted on escorting someone else, and since he chose Miss Lydia Hamilton, my brother had to escort Lady Rachel because she was the only other lady in the room he wasn't related to."

"Oh yes. Rachel and Lydia told me about that. Lydia was happy with the change. In fact, when I hoped to see her the other day, I learned she ran off to marry Lord Quinton."

"You're jesting!"

"I'm afraid not. She and Lord Quinton are not in London at the moment."

"You don't say." Amelia shook her head in wonder. "Wait until Grant hears about this."

"He didn't have his heart set on marrying her, did he?"

"He only met her that evening. There wasn't any time for him to get his hopes up."

Carol relaxed. That was a relief. She'd hate to marry someone who was secretly pining away for another lady.

"Will your friend be upset when she learns that Reuben is my suitor?" Amelia asked.

Noting the worried tone in Amelia's voice, Carol hurried to assure her, "Rachel left London to marry her secret admirer."

"Really? She had a secret admirer? That sounds like fun."

"It was fun. We spent considerable time guessing who he might be. It turned out to be the butler."

Amelia gasped. "The butler?"

"I was shocked, too. It sounds like the two left in a rush. I suppose they were afraid her brother might try to stop them."

"He could still do that when they return since he's her guardian."

"He won't. When he wrote to let me know what happened, he also told me he planned to go to Gretna Green to attend the wedding."

Amelia smiled. "That's really nice of him to allow the marriage. It's not common for a noblewoman to marry beneath her station. However, if this butler adored her from afar, I'm sure she'll be happy with him. What lady wouldn't be happy with someone who adores her?"

Carol nodded her agreement and drank the rest of the tea. She'd be thrilled if she could marry someone who adored her, but she was perfectly fine with marrying someone who didn't resent her. Even if Grant didn't love her, he was much better than the Duke of Augustine. Once she married Grant, she was going to wear colors again. She was only in her dark colors because her uncle made her wear them. She didn't see anything about the duke's death to mourn, and quite frankly, she didn't care what the rest of London had to say about it.

"Before the gentlemen come in here, I want to share something else with you," Amelia said. "Grant doesn't tell me much about his first wife, but there wasn't much of a relationship between them. You shouldn't worry that he'll compare you to her and find you lacking." She paused. "I wasn't sure what I thought of my brother rushing to propose to you since we didn't know you, but I have a good feeling about you. I think you'll make him happy. After all he's been through, he could use some happiness."

It was on the tip of Carol's tongue to ask her why he hadn't been happy, but she decided against it. It was probably best not to inquire about it so soon. She would find out more soon enough. She could only hope that Grant was as good as he seemed.

***

Carol's stomach was filled with butterflies as she walked through the menagerie with Grant, Lucinda, and Amelia. Last evening had gone well. After Grant and Reuben joined her and Amelia in the drawing room, the four ended up playing cards. Usually, Carol didn't care much for cards, but doing something with her hands helped to ease her nerves. It also helped that the three did most of the talking. She couldn't think of much to contribute to the conversation, but then, she was used to listening more than she talked. She could only hope no one thought she was as strange as her uncle did.

"That's a tiger," Amelia told Lucinda as they stopped at a cage. "It has all of those pretty stripes."

"I don't know if I'd say a beast like that has pretty stripes," Grant said. "If that thing was out of its cage, it could harm someone."

"What word would you use to describe the stripes?" Amelia asked.

He thought for a moment. "Noble. Yes, noble stripes fit an animal like that much better." He glanced at Carol. "What do you think?"

"You can't make her choose between us," Amelia argued. "That's not fair. I'll concede to your point. The tiger is a large animal, and as such, noble is a more fitting word to describe it."

"Can ride?" Lucinda asked.

Amelia laughed. "Heavens, no. It's not a horse."

"'Orse." Lucinda pointed to a zebra. "Ride?"

"Well, it is like a horse, but I don't know if it's meant to be ridden like one." Amelia glanced at Grant and Carol. "Do you know anything about zebras?"

"The plaque on its cage says this one came from the grasslands of East Africa," Grant replied.

When Amelia looked at her, Carol shrugged. "I never even heard of a zebra until today."

"I like the stripes," Amelia commented. "They seem to form a pattern. The same is true for the tiger."

"Want ride," Lucinda spoke up. "'Orse."

"We'll have to do that when you're older," Grant told her. "The kind of horse you're talking about isn't a toy like the wooden one you have."

"I probably shouldn't have given her that rocking horse as a gift, but I thought it was such an interesting toy when I saw it in the shop," Amelia explained to Carol. "The gentleman who made it assured me the thing would be suitable for a child her age."

"She gets plenty of use from it," Grant assured his sister. "It was a good gift."

The four moved to the next cage and saw a monkey swinging to its heart's content.

"Want that," Lucinda said.

"You want a monkey?" Grant asked.

"I think she means she wants the thing that monkey is swinging on," Amelia said.

Carol studied the girl's face and was struck by how happy she was. She enjoyed spending time with her father and aunt.

These people were good to her. They gave her a home where she felt loved and cared for. Grant and Amelia got along well, too. It reminded her of the close relationship Rachel had with her brother. Lydia wasn't as close to her brothers as Rachel was to hers, but Lydia got along well with them. Carol had never told her friends how much she envied them the relationship they had with their siblings.

Growing up, her father had doted on her, but he'd been taken from her too soon, and she'd felt alone in that townhouse ever since. Carol turned her attention back to Lucinda and smiled. She had made a good decision in accepting Grant's proposal. This was a home where one could feel comfortable. This marriage just might be the best thing that ever happened to her.

Chapter Six

On her wedding day, Carol decided to wear a silver gown. She knew her uncle wouldn't be pleased when he saw her choice in color, so she bypassed the drawing room and went straight to the front door as the coachman carried her trunk to the carriage.

Her uncle, unfortunately, happened to see her and grabbed her by the arm before she could slip out of the townhouse. "What do you think you're wearing?"

Without looking in his direction, she said, "I'm wearing a gown suitable for a wedding."

"It is not suitable. Go back and change into a darker color."

"I can't. All of my things are packed."

"Then we'll bring the trunk back in here so you can put on a different gown."

All the built-up tension she'd been under ever since he took over as her guardian erupted, and she snapped, "No! I'm free of you. You can't tell me what to do anymore."

He jerked her against him and glowered at her. "How dare you treat me with such insolence?"

She'd had enough of this. She was done cowering in front of him. Today, Grant was setting her free. Even if he didn't love her, he was good to his sister and his daughter. He would, no doubt, be much better to her than her uncle was. She pushed him away from her and hurried out of the townhouse before he could stop her. So she wouldn't have to be in the carriage alone with him, she bolted in the direction that would take her to

Grant's townhouse. If her uncle ruined her things out of spite, she would get new things.

She didn't bother glancing over her shoulder until she was halfway down the street. As she'd hoped, her uncle didn't bother following her. He only stood in the doorway of the townhouse with a scowl on his face and his hands on his hips. Just his look alone shot a shiver through her. Well, never mind that. He couldn't do anything to her once she was married. She turned around and continued down the street.

By the time she made it to Grant's townhouse, her heart was pounding. She had to wait for her heart rate to return to normal before she knocked on the door. When the footman asked about her trunk, she told him the carriage would be coming soon. If it didn't come because her uncle made the coachman dispose of it, she'd figure out what to say later.

She was glad to see the ceremony was going to be a small affair. Only Grant, Amelia, and Lucinda were in the drawing room with the vicar. She didn't know if she could manage it if there was a large number of people in attendance. Her nerves were already on edge. Would her uncle still come? Would he decide to stay home? If he came, would he tell them the story about how rebellious she was? People often believed a gentleman's word over a lady's, especially when that gentleman was older.

"Mama!" Lucinda called out and ran over to her.

Carol stopped in surprise as the girl held her arms up to her. After a moment, she realized the girl wanted her to pick her up. She hurried to do as she wished, hoping the others didn't notice how inept she was when it came to figuring out what people, especially those she barely knew, wanted.

Grant approached her. "You're early."

"I hope that's all right," Carol replied as Lucinda wrapped her arms around her neck.

"It's fine." Grant smiled and put his hand on the small of her back. "We're glad you're here." His gaze went to the doorway. "Is your uncle coming?"

Not wishing to tell him about the unpleasant confrontation she'd had with her uncle, she ventured, "He was following me when I left." She cleared her throat. "I'm a bit nervous about today. I thought a walk would help me relax."

"I'm nervous, too," Grant told her in a soft tone that was reserved only for her.

He was? He didn't look nervous. He looked confident.

"We'll wait for your uncle." He glanced between her and Lucinda then smiled. "She's taken an immediate liking to you. I'm glad."

She offered a tentative smile in return. "I'm glad, too. I don't have any experience with children. I hope I'll be all right as a mother."

"I have a feeling you'll do just fine."

She wished she had his assurance. It was easy to doubt herself when she was used to being criticized by her uncle. It hadn't helped that the Duke of Augustine had found her so repulsive that he hung himself in order to get out of marrying her.

"Since we're to wait for the Duke of Havre, would everyone like some tea?" Grant asked the group.

"I wouldn't mind something," the vicar spoke up. "My throat is a little parched."

"I'll get some tea at once. Is black all right?" Grant glanced at everyone.

Carol followed everyone's lead and nodded.

As Grant went to summon someone to bring the tea, Amelia told the vicar, "Why didn't you say you were thirsty? We would have been happy to bring in some tea."

The vicar answered, but Carol's mind went to her uncle. How long would they wait for him to arrive? She went over to a window and peered down the street. She didn't see any signs of his carriage yet.

"Want child?" Lucinda asked.

Carol forced her gaze to the girl in her arms who was looking up at her as if she had been waiting for her all of her life. "Are you asking if I want a child?"

Lucinda nodded.

Every child should feel accepted and loved. No one should end up feeling like she did after her father died. She couldn't do anything about her past, but she could do something about Lucinda's future.

With a smile, Carol said, "Yes, I do want a child." And she was going to be the kind of mother who was going to make this particular child feel accepted and loved.

By the way Lucinda's face brightened, Carol was assured she'd made the right reply. Well, this was nice. If Lucinda was going to keep letting her know when she said and did the right thing, then it was going to ease a lot of her apprehension about being a mother.

"Want Mama," Lucinda told her then rested her head on her shoulder.

Something in Carol warmed in response. Grant had told her that Lucinda didn't remember her mother since the lady had died shortly after giving birth to her. What an unfortunate thing. But it was something she and Lucinda had in common. Her mother hadn't lived long after she was born, either.

Amelia approached them. "It looks like you two are getting along well."

Lucinda lifted her head from Carol's shoulder, and Carol turned her gaze to Amelia.

Amelia offered them an apologetic smile. "I probably shouldn't have interrupted, but the tea is here if you want some."

Carol gave one more look down the street. She still didn't see her uncle's carriage. She released her breath then followed Amelia and sat next to Grant on the settee.

"How long will we wait for my uncle?" Carol forced out.

"I imagine he'll be here any minute since he was going to the carriage when you left." Grant paused as he handed her a cup. "That's odd. He should have arrived before you did if he took the carriage."

"Oh, well, I was ready to go, and he wasn't." Hoping they wouldn't push her for more information, Carol took a sip of the tea.

Grant offered Lucinda some tea, but she declined the offer and kept her head on Carol's shoulder. Thankfully, Amelia asked the vicar if he had anything else happening later that day, and since the vicar was a talker, the conversation that ensued allowed Carol some time to relax.

The vicar rambled for a good ten minutes, maybe a minute or two more. Just when Carol was beginning to think her uncle wasn't going to attend the wedding, he showed up. She had to swallow the bile that rose up in her throat as she rose to her feet to join the others in welcoming him.

Lucinda lifted her head and gave her a curious look. Carol hurried to smile in order to hide her uncertainty. Would her uncle start screaming at her? Would he warn Grant not to marry her? Would he pick her up and run her off to a convent so she could never see her friends again?

Her uncle took off his hat and gave everyone a pleasant smile. "Forgive me for being late. I had something to tend to at the last minute."

Grant urged him to come over to them. "We're glad you came. We were waiting for you."

Her uncle glanced her way, but she averted her gaze so she didn't have to make eye contact with him.

"I wouldn't miss this wedding for the world," her uncle said.

She managed not to shudder as she hurried over to the vicar.

Amelia put a reassuring hand on Carol's arm.

Carol's eyes grew wide. Did Amelia pick up on the tension between her and her uncle?

Amelia whispered, "My brother will be good to you."

Oh good. Amelia thought Carol was nervous about marrying Grant. She could handle that much better than the others knowing she detested her uncle. Carol managed a tentative glance in his direction. He took his place behind her and Grant. Amelia joined him. So that was it then? It was going to be this easy? Her uncle wasn't going to make this wedding difficult for her?

Since her uncle didn't bother looking in her direction, she gathered that everything was going to be all right. More than a little relieved, she turned her attention to the vicar so he could start the ceremony.

Chapter Seven

Carol sat in front of the vanity. It was time for bed. Her lady's maid had just left, and all there was to do at this point was wait for her wedding night. Her new lady's maid was considerably older than her with three grown children, and she had told Carol that she wouldn't be needing anything formal to wear to bed that evening. Carol was too embarrassed by her lack of knowledge to respond. She just turned her back to the lady's maid and let her slip the robe over her arms and shoulders. And now, she remained at the vanity, even though she was only wearing a robe.

Carol assumed Grant would come to this room since he was the gentleman in the relationship. He'd also been married before. He knew what to do. She didn't. While she waited, she let her mind go back over the day.

The day had started off shaky since she'd had the confrontation with her uncle on her way out the door. Thankfully, things had smoothed out afterward. She supposed her uncle hadn't wanted to look like a bad person in front of the others, so he'd remained pleasant all through the wedding breakfast. After that, he left, and she was informed that the maid was unpacking her things in her new bedchamber. She had to make herself wait until it was time to change gowns so she could sort through her things to make sure her uncle hadn't tampered with them. Fortunately, he hadn't. All of her things were still there, and they were in good condition.

The rest of the day had been nice. She'd played cards with Grant and Amelia while Lucinda napped, and then the four of them went for a stroll through Hyde Park. When they returned, it was time to get ready for dinner, and they had decided to play charades. Amelia, by far, was the more outgoing of the two siblings. She led most of the conversation. And that was fine with her. The more others talked, the less pressure she had in trying to figure out what to say.

A knock at the door separating her bedchamber from Grant's brought her back to the present. She took a deep breath and rose to her feet. This was it. She was about to find out what happened to a lady on her wedding night.

She opened the door and saw that Grant was also wearing a robe. Well, it was good her lady's maid had thought to put her in one, so she was appropriately attired.

"Is this a good time to come in?" Grant asked.

Realizing she hadn't moved out of his way, she quickly shifted aside so he could enter the room. "Yes, of course." She cleared her throat. "You'll have to forgive me. I've never had a gentleman in my bedchamber. I don't know what to do." Heat rushed up her cheeks. Was it wise to admit such a thing?

He offered her a reassuring smile. "I realize that embarrasses you, but it shouldn't. I'm glad you don't know what to expect. I like knowing I'm your first."

She didn't know why that should please him so much. Did all husbands think the same as Grant?

"I want you to know that the day was a wonderful one," he said. "I couldn't have planned it better if I'd tried. Thank you for being good to Lucinda."

Feeling some of her nerves ease, she returned his smile. "She's a sweet girl. I like her."

"She likes you, too. My sister says that children have a sense about people. They can tell if someone is good or not.

The Duke of Creighton's advice was for me to marry you. I owe him a favor for making such a worthy recommendation."

It'd been a long time since someone other than her friends had spoken so highly of her. This time when warmth came over her, it was with pleasure. "Thank you. I'll do what I can to be a good wife and mother."

He cupped the side of her face in his hand then bent forward to kiss her. His lips were warm and soft. The kiss was so brief that it seemed more like a caress than an actual kiss, but it made her tingle from the tip of her head all the way down to the tips of her toes all the same.

"Can I take you to the bed?" he whispered.

Swallowing the lump in her throat, she nodded. He took her hand and brought her to the bed. While he pulled back the blankets, she did her best to calm down. She never liked being anxious about things. She preferred knowing exactly what was going to happen. She wiped her hands on her robe and hoped the candlelight was dim enough to hide the fact that her hands were trembling.

Grant removed his robe, and at once, she scanned his body. She couldn't help it. As soon as she saw the thing sticking out between his legs, she couldn't help but wonder what it was. She had nothing like that between her legs.

When he turned toward her, she quickly averted her gaze. He didn't notice that she'd been staring at him, did he? If he did, he didn't mention it. Instead, he offered to help her out of her robe. She hurried to loosen the straps then turned her back so he could slip it off of her shoulders. He tossed the robe to the floor next to his robe then encouraged her to turn back around so she was facing him.

Without thinking, her gaze went back to that thing between his legs, and her eyes grew wide. It was bigger than before. Thankfully, he didn't ask her anything because her throat was so dry that she couldn't speak. He picked her up in his arms and placed her in the center of the bed. He got in beside her and pulled the blankets over them both.

Then he caressed her cheek with the back of his fingers and whispered, "You're a very beautiful lady, Carol."

His gaze was so tender that her breath caught in her throat. Before she could make sense of how she was feeling, he brought his mouth to hers. This kiss was longer than the one by the door. After ending that kiss, he proceeded to kiss her cheek. Then he kissed the side of her neck, which was surprisingly sensitive. When his lips returned to her mouth, she was able to enjoy it much more because she didn't feel as nervous as she'd been before.

He drew her closer to him. On instinct, she wrapped her arms around his neck. He moaned and brushed her bottom lip with his tongue. Not sure what he wanted, she hesitated but then parted her lips for him. He entered her mouth and explored her more intimately. Well, this was quite nice. She had never heard of this kind of kissing. She'd thought all kisses were either on the cheek or on the lips. She didn't know a gentleman could slip his tongue into a lady's mouth. And if she had known, she wouldn't have expected it to be the pleasant experience it was turning out to be. She relaxed against him and wondered what other nice surprises were in store for her.

He spent considerable time kissing her. From time to time, he would kiss her cheeks and her neck then return to her mouth. After a while, she ventured to return the action and kissed his cheeks and his neck. She thought it was only fair to do it to him since she was enjoying his kisses. And he seemed to appreciate her efforts since he held her closer and traced her body with his hands.

Having never been touched so intimately before, she had to fight back the bout of shyness that rose up within her. He was her husband. Though it was a very private activity they were doing, he was supposed to do this to her. It was part of being married. Thank goodness she wasn't doing this with the Duke of Augustine. She didn't think she could tolerate him touching her this way. But with Grant, she didn't mind it at all. It was all right to be vulnerable with him. He seemed to genuinely like her, and he was being gentle. The duke would never have been gentle. Nor would he have taken things slowly in order to give her time to get used to this.

Grant lowered the blankets that had been covering them, an action which exposed her breasts to the cool air. He brought his mouth to her shoulder and kissed it then proceeded to leave a trail of kisses to one of her breasts. A surge of pleasure coursed through her, and she lightly squeezed his arm. She didn't know where such a bold action on her part came from, but he let out a moan that let her know he liked it. He cupped her breast in his hand then traced her nipple with his tongue. She inwardly gasped. That was most pleasant indeed. She squeezed his arm harder, and he, in turn, continued to tease her nipple in a way that made her feel even better. It made her feel so good, in fact, that the last of her shyness departed. In its place was the desire to keep going, to find out where all of this was going.

She soon lost track of time. He fondled one breast then the other. He teased her with that tongue of his, using a technique she was certain was meant to arouse her. He had been married before. She hadn't. Naturally, he knew what he was doing, and he was doing it for her. This wasn't going to be something he did solely for himself. He cared about whether or not she enjoyed this act. And that made her like him all the more.

At some point, Grant decided to proceed lower on her body. She opened her eyes in surprise and watched as he kissed her stomach and then her abdomen. He couldn't mean to...? Surely, gentlemen didn't do that sort of thing.

But he moved in a way that let her know he wanted to be between her legs. She hurried to widen her legs so he could do as he wished. Then she watched with a mixture of excitement and shock as he knelt in front of her. He was going to put his mouth there. There—of all places! The moment his tongue found her sensitive nub, she cried out in pleasure and grabbed the sheets under her. That was a most unexpected—but intensely wonderful—surprise.

He slid a couple of fingers into her. This only added to her pleasure. She had no idea this area of her body was capable of feeling such pleasure. He began stroking her core in earnest while his tongue teased her sensitive nub. It really was wonderful. At the moment, there was nothing she wanted to do more than allow him to keep doing this to her. She closed her eyes and gave in to the moment.

She spread her legs further, and he went deeper inside her. His actions were sure and steady. She grabbed his shoulders and urged him to keep going. The tension mounting up within her core kept building toward something she'd never experienced before but needed more than she'd ever needed anything. He seemed to like tormenting her this way since he urged to her get "there". She wasn't sure where "there" was until the tension gave way to a burst of pleasure that consumed her. She cried out and grew completely still. It was so intense. She could do nothing but let each wave of pleasure crash into her, each one less intense than the one that came before it.

He waited until she had fully relaxed before he knelt over her. She was too weak to do more than take him into her. There was a sting that momentarily brought her out of her state of bliss. He remained still, his body taut as he waited for her to adjust to him.

"Carol?" he whispered, his voice tense with need.

She shifted until the sting significantly diminished. "It's all right. You can move."

He gave her a long kiss that warmed her heart. He hadn't meant to hurt her. It was something that probably couldn't be helped since she hadn't been with a gentleman before. She kissed him in return then wrapped her legs around his waist. The action gave him more room, and the last of the pain ebbed.

"Thank you," he whispered then kissed her ear.

She didn't know what he was thanking her for, but he was soon moving inside her, and that brought her attention back to what they were doing.

He continued to move slowly inside her and continued until his movements were more urgent. She held onto him, noting the way his body grew more tense with each thrust. Then, there was the moment when he went still and let out a cry, and a pleasant warmth filled her. It wasn't until he collapsed in her arms that she realized it was over.

So this was what husbands and wives did in secret. This was how ladies conceived children. Now that it was over, she could finally piece everything together. After a few moments, she decided this was quite lovely. The act of joining their bodies in bed was a pleasurable event. In the future, she would know what to expect, and, better yet, she would look forward to it.

He lifted himself on his elbows and stroked her chin with his fingers. "Do you mind if I sleep in here with you?"

The bout of shyness returning, she said, "It would be nice if you did."

He smiled in a way that let her know her answer made him happy. He kissed her for a while before he got off of her, pulled the blankets on top of them, and drew her into his arms. He was warm and strong. She liked that. She felt protected and safe.

He fell asleep before she did, but she didn't mind. It gave her time to enjoy how exciting it was to be with someone who was going to treat her well. She was glad she married him. He was nothing like the Duke of Augustine, and she liked that most about him.

Chapter Eight

When Grant woke up the next morning, he was aroused.

Last night had been wonderful. More wonderful than he could have ever imagined being with a lady could be. He'd known his first wife had been cold, but it hadn't occurred to him just how cold she'd been until he made love to Carol.

Fiona had been his first, but she hadn't been his. He hadn't realized she hadn't been a virgin until he sought out books on how to be adequate in bed. That book taught him the differences between a virgin and an experienced lady. Carol had been a virgin. He'd had to push through her maidenhead. He had no way of knowing when Fiona lost hers. He hadn't asked, and she hadn't volunteered the information. To this day, he didn't want to know. It was enough to know that Carol hadn't been with another gentleman. She had saved herself for marriage, and that endeared him to her in ways he could never properly express to another person.

He wanted to make love to her this morning. He didn't want to wait for tonight, but considering that last night had been her first time, he had to allow her body time to heal. He owed it to her to be the kind of gentleman worthy of her. If he could stay true to his wedding vows when Fiona hadn't, he could do this small thing for Carol.

Since she was still asleep in his arms, he had to be careful as he got out of the bed. He briefly noted the spot of dried blood on the sheet, further proving Carol's innocence. The fire in the fireplace had fizzled out at some point during the night. The cool air was actually a welcome relief. It helped to calm his ardor. Even so, he didn't want Carol to get cold. He pulled the blankets up to her neck to keep her warm.

After he retrieved his robe off the floor, he gave one more look at Carol and smiled. It was nice to feel good about being intimate with someone for a change. He slipped into his room and shut the door softly between their bedchambers so he wouldn't wake her. Then he got ready for the day.

He was usually in the drawing room before Amelia, but on this morning, she was sitting in a chair with a card in her hand.

"Is something wrong?" he asked, noting the frown on her face.

She looked up from the card and shrugged. "I received a request from a suitor to pay me a visit later today."

He sat next to her. "You don't seem all that excited about it."

"The suitor is Mr. Everson."

Really? He was sending another card? "Didn't he come by twice this week already?"

She nodded. "I was hoping this was from Reuben. We had such a good time at the dinner party. He asked if he could come by for a visit, but I haven't received anything from him yet."

"Maybe he doesn't want to seem too eager." He gestured to the card in her hand. "You're not all that pleased with Mr. Everson because he wants to see you all the time."

"Mr. Everson doesn't interest me like Reuben does. If it was Reuben, I'd want to see him every day."

"That must be true since you refer to Reuben so intimately. You know Mr. Everson's Christian name, but you never use it."

She set the card down and slumped in her chair. "I ought to tell Mr. Everson I don't want to see him anymore."

"I don't know if that's wise. He's wealthy and kind. He's never said or done anything the least bit scandalous. A gentleman like that would honor his wedding vows."

"But he's boring. There's nothing about him that makes him stand out from the others."

Grant resisted the urge to grimace. Like poor Mr. Everson, ladies considered him boring as well. He didn't have the wit and charm other gentlemen did. Choosing his words carefully, he said, "Just because a gentleman doesn't attract a lot of people, it doesn't mean he'll make a bad husband."

"I realize that, but is it wrong for me to want to be with someone who appeals to me? Reuben has a marvelous sense of humor. I had no interest in learning about fishing before I met him, but the stories he tells captivate me so much that I want to learn more about it."

"You have every right to want to be entertained when you talk to someone," Grant allowed. "Is Mr. Everson really that tedious?"

She thought for a long moment. "I don't know how to explain it. When Reuben is around, I feel alive. There's something that seems to spark between us. When I'm with Mr. Everson, I don't feel anything." She paused. "I hate to say it, but Lord Compton doesn't interest me that much, either."

"He doesn't?" Grant found that surprising since Lord Compton had made the entire room laugh when they went to his dinner party.

"I know Lord Compton can tell good stories. It's just that spark isn't there with him, either. I only agreed to the courtships with Mr. Everson and Lord Compton because you wanted me to seem attractive to all of the gentlemen out there."

"Well, it doesn't hurt to let the gentlemen know you could have anyone you want."

If he had made Fiona think he could have other ladies before their marriage, she might not have taken him for granted the way she did. Maybe she would have tried to get to know him. Maybe she wouldn't have run off to secretly visit the gentlemen who already had ladies vying for them. He forced the past aside. He didn't want to think of how Fiona saw him. This was the day after the most wonderful night of his life. He'd rather focus on the future he might have with Carol.

"I hope Reuben asks to pay me a visit soon," Amelia said. "Waiting for him to see me is driving me to distraction. You don't suppose that's what he's trying to do, do you? Maybe he thinks by making me wait, I'll want him even more."

If that's what Reuben was thinking, he was right. The longer Amelia had to wait for him, the more she seemed to long for him.

"Maybe we should have another dinner party and invite him to it," Amelia pressed.

"We can't do that so soon," Grant replied. "It would be awkward. I'll take you to the next ball, and you can have two dances with him."

"If he's there. He doesn't go to all of the balls."

"Not everyone does. I'm only going to them now because you're in your Season. The next ball is tomorrow evening. I believe Lord Worsley is hosting it."

Her eyes lit up. "Reuben will surely be at that one! Lord Worsley and Reuben's brother are friends."

"How do you know so much about Reuben?"

A blush creeping up her cheeks, she said, "I might have asked around about him and his family after we met him at that dinner party."

Grant relaxed. He was starting to worry she was stalking the poor gentleman.

"London is a small place," Amelia continued. "A lot of people know each other. It's not difficult to find out about someone."

"Apparently not."

Amelia gestured to him that someone was coming into the room, so he hurried to his feet. He pushed aside his disappointment when he realized it wasn't Carol.

The butler came into the room and poured tea into their cups. Grant glanced at the clock. It was almost nine. Lucinda would be down soon. He didn't think Carol would be asleep much longer. Recalling the condition of her bedsheets, he excused himself and found one of the laundry maids to ask her to make sure they were washed. He didn't know if the maids could remove the telltale sign of Carol's virginity from the sheets, but there was no harm in trying. When he returned to the drawing room, Amelia was drinking her tea.

"Where did you run off to?" she asked.

"I just wanted to talk to one of the maids about doing some laundry." He cleared his throat as he returned to his chair. "What do you plan to do today? Don't tell me you're going to follow poor Reuben around London."

She chuckled. "No, I'm not going to follow Reuben around London. I'm more subtle than that. I think I'll shop for a new book to read. Then this afternoon, I'll have to see Mr. Everson." Her gaze went to him. "I don't suppose you can spare Carol so she can be here, too?"

He didn't hide his disappointment. "I want to spend the day with her."

"You can have her for most of the day. I only need her from two to three. That's when Mr. Everson plans to be here."

He sighed. "I suppose I can let you have her for an hour."

"Thank you!" She gave him a quick kiss on the cheek then sat back in her chair. "I don't recall you being this excited about spending time with your first wife. But then, she liked to stay in the country a lot. I know you went to visit her as much as you could, but when you're the earl of an estate, you need to be in London most of the time. So when you think about it, you two rarely ever saw each other."

He decided not to tell her why he had chosen to stay in London. Let her think he had important investments that needed his attention all the time. It was better than telling her the truth. It was an arrangement that had worked well for him and Fiona.

"Papa, Auntie Ama!"

Surprised he hadn't heard the maid approach with Lucinda, Grant rose to his feet. He needed to keep his mind in the present. It did no good to dwell on the past. Not only did he hate thinking of it, but it stopped him from being at his best.

Lucinda stopped just short of them and looked around the room as the maid left. "Mama?"

"She's upstairs," Grant told her as he sat back down. "Come, have a seat and drink some tea."

Lucinda nodded and joined him. He filled the cup halfway so that the girl wouldn't spill the drink and gave it to her.

"I bet your mama is getting ready for breakfast," Amelia told Lucinda. "I know she's looking forward to seeing you." She glanced at Grant. "Will you three do something special today?"

He shrugged. "I'm not sure what else we can do except go for a walk." Lucinda was too young to play games.

"Want lion," Lucinda said.

He frowned. "But we were at the menagerie earlier this week."

"Animals fun," Lucinda replied, not the least bit bothered by going again so soon.

"There wouldn't be any harm in going again," Amelia commented. "Just as long as you can be here at two."

"Why two?" Lucinda asked.

For someone so young, the girl sure did pick up a lot of what was going on around her, which was why Grant was careful not to say anything bad about Fiona in front of her. He didn't want Lucinda to think badly about Fiona. A girl ought to think well of the lady who gave her life. As long as she was developing a good relationship with Carol, that was the important thing.

"One of my suitors is coming here at two," Amelia told Lucinda.

Grant noted the tone in his sister's voice, so he said, "I hope you'll do a better job of showing more interest in him when he's here."

"I'll do my best," Amelia promised.

This time he heard the person who approached the room. He got to his feet in time for Carol to step through the threshold. At once, warmth swept over him. She was even lovelier to look at this morning than she'd been yesterday.

She offered them an apologetic smile. "I'm sorry I slept in so late. I hope I didn't keep everyone waiting for breakfast."

He took her by the arm and led her over to the others. "No, we aren't ready for breakfast quite yet. Lucinda was just saying she'd like to go to the menagerie again. I don't suppose you'd be interested in returning there?"

"I'd love to go back," Carol said. "I had a lot of fun there the other day."

Lucinda cheered and started bouncing like a ball.

Grant shook his head. "It's all right to be excited, but you don't want to show too much excitement. A simple smile will do."

Lucinda stopped bouncing, but Grant could tell it was difficult for her to stay still since she was fidgeting.

"Is it that bad she shows her excitement?" Carol asked.

Amelia giggled. "Can you imagine what gentlemen would say if ladies jumped up and down around them? I think we'd look silly."

Grant held his tongue. It wouldn't be appropriate for him to tell Carol he'd like to see her jump up and down in front of him. She had nice round breasts. No doubt, they'd look quite nice bouncing in her gown. But something like that should be reserved in private.

Before he allowed himself the fantasy—and ended up with an erection right in front of everyone—he offered Carol a seat then gave her some tea. "We'll go to the menagerie after we eat." Turning to Lucinda, he picked her up and set her on his lap. "Do you want more to drink?"

Lucinda shook her head.

"I'm looking forward to going back to the menagerie," Carol said. "Would you believe I've never been there until we went? I had no idea there were so many exotic animals."

"Did you not have an interest in seeing them before?" Amelia asked.

Carol paused before saying, "No, I had an interest. I just didn't have the opportunity to go."

What was Carol not telling them? Surely, she had hesitated to answer Amelia's question for a reason. He debated whether or not he should ask. There were plenty of things he'd rather not tell anyone. Carol probably had some secrets, too. It might be best not to pry. The last thing he wanted to do was make her uncomfortable, especially after the night they'd shared together.

Amelia, not picking up on Carol's hesitation, said, "At two, I'll need you here. Mr. Everson will come by, and the visit will go by faster if we can play cards."

Before Carol could ask, Grant filled in, "Mr. Everson is one of her suitors." Unable to resist the urge to tease her, he continued, "My poor sister entertains quite a few of them. It's gotten to the point where she's bored."

Amelia shook her head at him. "That's terrible for you to say, Grant. It's not like that." With a glance at Carol, she amended, "Not all of them. Let me tell you about them."

Amelia started to explain what all of her suitors were like. Since Grant already knew about them, he let his mind wander to what his marriage to Carol might be like, and for the first time in a very long time, he felt good about the future.

57

Chapter Nine

Carol enjoyed her visit to the menagerie with Grant and Lucinda more the second time around. This time, she didn't have to worry that Grant might change his mind about the marriage at the last moment and find a way out of it, just like the Duke of Augustine had. But he hadn't. He had been at the townhouse waiting for her with the vicar, and he had said his vows. Her future was secure. She'd never have to worry about her uncle ever again. For the first time since her father was alive, she felt like she wasn't being criticized over every little thing she said and did. So she spent more time studying the animals and noticed how each one was unique.

"Did you know that no two zebras have the same exact pattern of stripes?" a gentleman asked as he approached them.

Grant glanced Carol's way as if to ask if she knew him. She shook her head in response. She had never seen this person before. Perhaps it was the owner of the menagerie. The person who had collected their money at the entrance had been too young to be the owner of such an elaborate enterprise.

Grant turned his gaze back to the middle-aged gentleman. "No, we didn't know that."

"Well, it's true," the gentleman said. "Allow me to introduce myself. I'm Mr. Weber."

After a moment, Grant replied, "I'm Lord Wright. This is my wife and our daughter. My apologies, but do we know each other?"

"No," Mr. Weber began, "none of us were acquainted before today. I just noticed you looking at the zebra and thought I'd tell you something interesting about it."

Grant relaxed. "We wouldn't have guessed each zebra has a different pattern of stripes."

"Most people don't. I happen to do a lot of reading about animals, so I know these little facts about them. For instance, ostriches are birds that can't fly. They can, however, run faster than either one of us. If that ostrich over there were to get out of its cage, we wouldn't be able to catch it."

Carol and Grant glanced at the cage Mr. Weber pointed to. Lucinda, who had probably grown bored of the conversation, was checking out the animal in the next cage. Carol didn't blame her. She enjoyed looking at the animals but wasn't all that concerned with their stripes or how fast they could run.

"Do you come to this menagerie often?" Mr. Weber asked.

"No," Grant replied, his tone indicating that he thought the gentleman's question was odd. "This is our second time."

"I come here twice a month," Mr. Weber said. "I like to see what new animals they add to the exhibit. I used to come here with my wife, but alas, I am now widowed. We were just as happy as you and your wife appear to be. She was a lovely lady. Our courtship was mostly kept private until we were permitted to marry. The wait was well worth it."

Why was he sharing this with people he just met? And why was he glancing at her as if he was trying to expose some deep, dark secret he was sure she was hiding? Carol shifted closer to Grant, and she was glad when he placed his hand comfortingly under her elbow for support.

"I'm sorry to hear that." Grant reached over and took Lucinda's hand. "I hate to end this conversation, but we were just on our way home. We hope you enjoy the rest of your visit here."

Mr. Weber stepped aside and tipped his hat. "It was a pleasure to make your acquaintance."

Grant offered a quick nod then led Carol and Lucinda out of the menagerie.

Lucinda tugged on his arm to go back into the menagerie. "Papa, more."

Carol glanced back at the entrance of the menagerie and saw that Mr. Weber was watching them. Specifically, he was watching her. She quickly averted her gaze. There was something wrong. She'd never seen Mr. Weber before. At least she didn't remember him if she had. Her uncle would bring friends and business acquaintances over, but she was certain that Mr. Weber hadn't been one of them. Perhaps he'd seen her at a ball. She'd been to quite a few of those, and a lot of gentlemen attended them. It was hard to keep track of all of the ones her uncle had made her dance with. When she dared a peek back, he was gone.

"Carol?" Grant asked.

Drawing her attention to Grant, she saw that he had settled Lucinda down so that she was no longer trying to go back to the menagerie.

"Don't mind him," Grant told her. "He's strange, but I don't think he'll bother us anymore. Let's go to the market. We can pick up candy for Lucinda, and if you find something of interest, you can get it."

Carol took one more look at the doorway of the menagerie and was relieved to see that Mr. Weber was no longer there. She turned her attention back to Grant and Lucinda. "Candy sounds nice."

"Candy!" Lucinda agreed, not hiding her excitement.

Chuckling, Grant said, "Candy it is then. We'll even pick some up for Amelia." With a smile that threatened to melt her right on the spot, he took her by the elbow and escorted her and Lucinda to the carriage.

***

Carol forced back a yawn as Mr. Everson went on and on about a dinner party he'd recently attended. She had no idea who the other people at the dinner party were. He'd given their names, but she'd given up on listening to him about fifteen minutes after he arrived. Instead, her mind wandered to when she'd get to see Grant again. She'd never been in love before, but she bet this longing she experienced to be with Grant was a good indication she was in love with him.

Amelia let out a laugh that, if Carol had to guess, was forced. Carol glanced her way.

"You ought to be good, Mr. Everson," Amelia said. "Sliding a card up your sleeve, even if you're not playing for money, is cheating."

He winked at her. "It's only cheating if you get caught. But I assure you that I only did it that one time. I don't make it a habit of playing tricks on others like that. I truly meant it as a joke."

The butler came into the room, and when Carol saw him look her way, she excused herself before going over to him.

"This came for you," he whispered and handed her a calling card from Rachel.

Rachel was back in London! Carol was so excited that she almost grabbed her hat and shawl so she could leave at once. She took a deep breath and calmed her enthusiasm. She could see Rachel after Mr. Everson left. She quietly thanked the butler then returned to the chair.

"I don't mean to brag, but I am one of the most knowledgeable gentlemen in town," Mr. Everson was telling Amelia. "I've been invited to give lectures at the *Society of Educated Gentlemen*. It's an exclusive club. Lord Cadwalader established it himself."

"That sounds exciting." Amelia's gaze went to Carol. "Doesn't that sound exciting?"

"Quite," Carol replied since it was the polite thing to say.

Carol was aware of that club. Her uncle hoped to join it. The fact that the Duke of Augustine had gotten accepted but he hadn't had irritated him to no end. If Carol guessed, one of the reasons he refused to release her from the marriage to the duke was in hopes that Lord Cadwalader would permit him access to the club. If not as a member, then as a guest. She supposed the duke's death must have come as a disappointment to him since he had no connection to it now.

She didn't want to acknowledge that part of her which was glad her uncle's hopes had been dashed. She wanted to be deserving of her friends. She wanted to be deserving of Amelia and Lucinda. Most of all, she wanted to be deserving of Grant. She finally had a life worth living. She couldn't let the poison of vengeance ruin things. She had always believed that good ultimately conquered the bad, and for that to happen, one had to think and behave uprightly.

"Did you hear that Lord and Lady Cadwalader welcomed another grandchild the other day?" Mr. Everson asked Amelia.

Amelia shook her head.

"It was a boy," he said. "They were relieved. Up to then, their son had nothing but girls. He has a total of five of them. So the boy came as a great relief to them. Naturally, they want the title to pass on to a grandson. If it doesn't go to a grandson, it'll go to Lord Cadwalader's nephew. They like their nephew enough, but he is a real spender. They don't want their family fortune to get squandered."

The butler came into the room with an apologetic expression on his face. Once more, Carol went over to him. He had another calling card, but this one was for Amelia. Carol checked for the sender and saw Reuben's name. She smiled.

Amelia would like this! She quietly thanked the butler and returned to her chair.

The visit, thankfully, didn't last much longer. Carol had a difficult time sitting still knowing that Amelia was going to get a chance to see Reuben again. As soon as Mr. Everson left, Amelia held the card out to her new friend.

Amelia took a look at it and shrieked in delight.

Carol laughed. "I thought you might like that card."

"You're right. I do. What a relief. I was beginning to fear that Reuben wasn't as interested in me as he let on at the dinner party." She paused. "The butler came in twice. Who is the other card for?"

"That one is for me. My friend Rachel returned to London." Carol hesitated. She didn't know how interested Amelia was in her life, but she didn't think it would hurt to make an offer for her to come along. "I plan to visit her. Would you like to go with me?"

Amelia nodded. "I'd love to see her again. I like her. I also like you. I doubt I would have survived this afternoon if you hadn't been here."

"I don't know how much I helped you. I was quiet most of the time."

"It was enough that you were here. You have no idea how much you eased my nerves around Mr. Everson. He's a fine gentleman, but I don't feel as comfortable with him as I do with Reuben. There's something about Reuben that makes me feel complete." She chuckled. "That must sound silly."

"I don't think it sounds silly. I think it sounds wonderful." That was how she felt with Grant. She felt as if Grant accepted her. He didn't judge her and find her lacking. She was truly his wife.

"Grant likes Rachel's brother. Perhaps we should all go there. I'll go to the library and ask him if he wants to join us.

After the tedious visit with Mr. Everson, it'll be nice to have someone we can look forward to seeing."

Before Carol could respond, Amelia hurried out of the room. Carol felt a grin tug at her lips. Amelia, it seemed, had a spontaneous side to her…when it wasn't hampered by someone she considered *tedious*. Eager to see Rachel, Carol decided to get her hat and shawl from her bedchamber so she'd be ready to leave the townhouse.

Chapter Ten

Carol stepped into her friend's townhouse. Grant and Amelia followed. She had expected to visit her friend after her marriage to the Duke of Augustine, but at that time, she thought she'd need a shoulder to cry on. It was better to be here under these circumstances.

"Did your friend really marry the butler?" Amelia whispered after the footman left them alone in the drawing room.

Carol nodded. "She did. I had no idea she had an interest in him." The last time she had spoken with Rachel, she'd thought Rachel was interested in Lord Swenson. Carol had to read through Horatio's missive five times before she realized that Rachel had married the butler instead.

"As long as Horatio approves, then there won't be any issues," Grant whispered. "And if Rachel is happy, that's a good thing."

"May we all be lucky to have a love match," Amelia agreed. "I think it's romantic."

Grant arched an eyebrow. "Are you telling me you have an attraction for our butler?"

Amelia's eyes grew wide. "Heavens no. There's only one gentleman I have my heart set on, and he's not the butler."

"Poor Mr. Everson has no idea you were thinking of Reuben the entire time he was trying to impress you," Carol commented.

Amelia turned her gaze to Grant. "I think I should let Mr. Everson and Mr. Compton know I've picked Reuben. It's not fair to make them think they might marry me."

Grant shook his head. "Wait until Reuben proposes. I know you're not all that excited about Mr. Everson or Mr. Compton, but they are decent gentlemen. They would make good husbands."

Carol noted the disappointment on Amelia's face as the footman came into the room with tea and scones. While she sympathized with Amelia, she couldn't blame Grant for being cautious. One couldn't predict what was going to happen. Look at her. She thought she was going to end up with the Duke of Augustine, but thankfully, she was with Grant instead.

Rachel's brother, Horatio, came into the room and greeted the three of them as the footman poured tea into their cups. "Did you take my advice and marry Lady Carol?" he asked Grant as he glanced her way.

"I did." Grant smiled at her in a way that made her body flood with warmth. "Thank you for the recommendation. It was the best one I ever received."

That comment was even better than the smile he had given her. Imagine her own husband saying he was happy with her! If she hadn't been excited to be with him before, she certainly was now. She caught the pleased grin on Amelia's face and knew her sister-in-law was satisfied with the match, too.

"I'm glad things worked out," Horatio said. "My sister will be down in a moment. She has been packing her things. She and Edwin will be moving to their own townhouse tomorrow." He paused. "It still feels strange to think of Edwin as my brother-in-law, but I'll get used to it. The two have a love match, and one couldn't ask for more than that." Horatio turned to Grant. "I have another recommendation for you, but it doesn't involve marriage. Lord Steinbeck and Mr. Jasper are going to take on a certain investment. I don't suppose you would be interested in joining me and Edwin in the library while the ladies stay here and talk? We won't be long. Maybe a half hour."

"I think I can spare a half hour from my bride," Grant said with another smile at Carol.

"Wonderful." Horatio turned to the footman and said, "Tell Mr. Morgan to meet us in the library."

The footman blinked for a moment before he gave an understanding nod and left the room.

Horatio whispered, "Mr. Morgan is Edwin. I think the servants aren't any more prepared for the change in his status than I was when I found out my sister ran off to Gretna Green with him." In a louder voice, he said, "If you ladies will excuse us, we're off to discuss railways."

Carol and Amelia nodded then waited for Grant and Horatio to leave before they settled on the settee.

"It's nice that your friend's brother has allowed her to marry the butler," Amelia said. "Some gentlemen would annul the union."

Carol picked up a cup of tea. "Horatio has always done everything he could to make Rachel happy." She took a sip of the hot liquid that had a hint of cinnamon in it. "They're more like close friends than brother and sister."

"I think that's lovely. I could tell the two were close when I met them at the dinner party."

"You and Grant get along well, too."

"Yes, we do, though that came about after Fiona's death. Growing up, I didn't see him a lot. He spent a lot of time acquiring money. Then when he married, he seemed to disappear into his library. There were days I didn't see him at all. It wasn't until after Lucinda was born that he came to me. I suppose since I'm a lady, he figured I would know what to do with a child, but I was just as lost as he was."

"You two manage fine with Lucinda. She's a delightful child."

"We had time to get used to raising her." Amelia chuckled. "If you had seen us when she was a baby, you would have laughed at how scared we were. We were certain that we were doing something wrong. Sometimes we still aren't certain we're doing things correctly, but as you said, she's a fine child."

Carol hesitated before saying, "It's not my place to pry, but why don't you hire someone to look after her for you? Most people do that."

"We thought about it, but Grant said Fiona was raised by her nanny, and he didn't want to risk Lucinda turning out like Fiona." She shrugged. "I don't really know more than that. Lucinda is his child, so we'll raise her the way he wants."

Carol nodded. "I want to do what he wants for Lucinda, too."

Amelia glanced at the door and rose to her feet. Carol turned and saw that Rachel was coming into the room. Carol couldn't believe the difference in Rachel. She'd never seen her friend look more radiant. It must be love. Love brought a glow to ladies' faces. She wondered if she had a similar glow to her face. She felt like she was falling in love. At the very least, she was very happy with Grant.

"I'm sorry I didn't let you know I was eloping," Rachel told Carol as she reached the two ladies. "I wanted to, but Edwin and I were in a hurry to get out of here in case my brother decided to stop us. I'm glad you received my calling card. So, you married Lord Wright?"

"I did," Carol replied as the three sat down. "Did you hear what happened to the Duke of Augustine?"

Rachel nodded. "My brother told me. What a shock."

"Yes, it was unexpected." Carol decided not to comment further since she didn't want Amelia to know how much she'd hated him. "Just as unexpected as your elopement."

Rachel laughed and put her hand over her heart. "Oh, I agree! Did you find out about Lydia?"

"Lydia ran off to the country with Lord Quinton," Carol replied.

Rachel laughed harder. "By choice. I think out of everyone, she shocked me the most. I wish you were here that evening when Horatio hosted that dinner party. You have no idea how awful the whole experience was. I felt terrible for Lord Wright. He was supposed to escort Lydia to dinner."

"Don't feel bad for Grant," Amelia inserted. "He's with Carol, and I think they make a wonderful match."

"That's good to hear," Rachel said. "My brother was afraid Lord Wright wouldn't want to talk to him after that dinner. I still can't believe Lydia fell in love with Lord Quinton after everything he did at the dinner."

The more Carol heard about the ordeal, the more she wished she had been there to witness it. It sounded like an entertaining evening.

"I think the more shocking thing is knowing you and the butler were secretly in love the whole time the dinner party was going on," Amelia said.

"Oh, I wasn't secretly in love with him then," Rachel replied. "I liked him, but I didn't fancy him in that way. All of that came later."

A worried frown crossed Amelia's face. "So you did fancy Mr. St. George that evening at the dinner party?"

"I thought I did at the time, but it was obvious he preferred you to me." Noting the deepening frown on Amelia's face, Rachel hurried to assure her, "It's all right. My interest in him stemmed from thinking he was my secret admirer. Once I realized he wasn't, I had no attachment to him at all."

"She means it," Carol added. "I was with her at the ball when she took an interest in Lord Swenson." She glanced at Rachel. "But he wasn't your secret admirer like you thought?"

Rachel shook her head. "No, he wasn't, and thank goodness for that. Edwin is much better. I can't imagine being this excited about anyone else. I just knew my secret admirer was the perfect match for me."

Amelia didn't hide her relief. "That puts my mind at ease. I was afraid to tell you that Mr. St. George is one of my suitors."

"He's her favorite suitor," Carol teased with a mischievous grin. A blush crept up Amelia's face, so she hurried to add, "And I suspect he fancies you above all other ladies."

"I think so, too," Rachel agreed. "He barely gave me or Belladonna a second glance all evening at the dinner party."

Amelia's face grew redder, but this time it seemed to stem from pleasure rather than being embarrassed.

Carol turned back to Rachel. "I don't know about Amelia, but I want to know all about you and Edwin. How did you find out he was your secret admirer? What did you do after finding out? How did you two decide to elope? What was your trip to Gretna Green like?"

Rachel chuckled. "You don't need to ask so many questions. I'll tell you everything." Picking up her cup of tea, she started to explain the whole story.

***

Grant accepted the glass of brandy from Horatio then sat in the leather chair near the fireplace. "You say this is a sound investment?"

Horatio poured brandy into two glasses. "If Lord Steinbeck and Mr. Jasper are excited about it, you can guarantee it. They aren't among London's wealthiest for no reason. I don't know what it is about them, but they seem to have the Midas touch."

Grant had heard such exhortation from other gentlemen. He'd also heard that they spent most of their time at White's. Not being a member of White's himself, he was unable to obtain an audience with them through that avenue. "Are you a member of White's?"

"I'm not, but I know Lord Quinton. Since Lord Quinton is a member of White's, he arranged for me to have a conversation with them. I hope my acquaintance with Lord Quinton is all right."

Surprised, Grant asked, "Why should it upset me?"

"Well, I know Lord Quinton made things difficult for you at my dinner party."

Grant chuckled. "Oh, that. While I do think Lord Quinton lacks the social graces, I'm very happy with Carol. I'm glad things worked out the way they did."

"You have no idea how relieved I am to hear that."

The door opened, and Horatio waved for the young gentleman to come into the room. "Grant, this is my brother-in-law, Edwin. Edwin, this is Grant." He gave Edwin a glass of brandy then gestured for him to have a seat near Grant.

Grant picked up on Edwin's uncertainty as he approached the chair. It was funny how he didn't remember Edwin when he was a butler, but then, servants in other people's households tended to blend into the background. "It must not be easy to make the adjustment from being a butler to being a duke's brother-in-law."

Edwin offered a smile as he settled into the chair. "I didn't realize my apprehension showed."

"Not everyone is good at hiding their emotions," Grant said. "That's not always a bad thing." He wished Fiona hadn't been skilled at pretending to be something she wasn't. If she hadn't been, he wouldn't have made the mistake of marrying her. It was only after the wedding that her mask came off, and by then, it was too late to do anything about it. He took a sip of the brandy to help ward off the chill that crept through him.

"You'll get used to your new station soon enough," Horatio assured Edwin as he settled into a chair next to them.

"My father thought you were one of the best servants he ever had. He said you adapted well to new situations."

"I thought the world of your father," Edwin told Horatio. "It was a privilege to work for him."

Horatio smiled. "If he was here now, he would approve of the union between you and my sister. All you need to do is build up your wealth so my nephews and nieces will have a comfortable life."

"That's not difficult to do," Grant inserted. "As long as you avoid getting into debt and making ridiculous wagers, you'll be better off than half of the gentlemen in London."

"Right," Horatio agreed. "It does no good to get impatient when it comes to building wealth. This is a slow and steady journey. And I promise you that Lord Steinbeck's and Mr. Jasper's advice won't steer any of us wrong. While I appreciate Lord Quinton's help in meeting them, I think it'll be safer to host this upcoming dinner party without him."

Edwin chuckled, and the two glanced his way. Edwin cleared his throat and straightened up in embarrassment.

Recalling that Edwin had witnessed the whole dinner since he'd been the butler at the time, Grant grinned. "Are you thinking that I'll kill Lord Quinton if I see him again?"

"Well…" Edwin's gaze went to Horatio, who seemed as if he was holding back his own laughter. "I've been a butler during plenty of dinner parties, and I can't think of a single one that went as poorly as that one did."

Grant hadn't thought about it, but he supposed the servants would have found the whole thing amusing. "Yes, I have a feeling that Lord Quinton is memorable, no matter where he goes."

They were silent for a moment then burst into laughter. Grant laughed so hard, he had to wipe tears from his eyes.

"Lord Quinton does make an impression," Horatio agreed. "I can only imagine what he's like at White's."

"I'm sure he manages better there since there aren't any ladies wearing a horrifying red gown or green-and-blue cameo," Grant said.

"No," Horatio began, "but he might bicker about something he is going to eat or drink."

"Do they eat in gentlemen's clubs?"

Horatio shrugged. "Maybe not, but they certainly drink."

"With Lord Quinton there, they would need to."

They laughed again.

Grant couldn't recall the last time he'd laughed for so long. It felt good. All of the weight he'd been carrying around with him for years seemed to be lifted somehow. Perhaps things really were turning around for the better.

"We do owe Lord Quinton some appreciation for this investment opportunity," Horatio spoke up once they managed to stop laughing. "Also, we're not completely rid of him. He ran off to marry one of Rachel's friends. Edwin, her friends visit her all the time. At some point, you're bound to have to entertain Lord Quinton in your home."

Grant offered a solemn nod. Then, after a moment, a joke came to mind, and for once he decided to say it. "You better warn your cook to make everything as bland as possible so Lord Quinton doesn't think you're trying to poison him."

They laughed again, and this time, they didn't try to stop.

Chapter Eleven

Grant sat impatiently in his bedchamber as he waited for the right moment to go to Carol's room. The lady's maid was still helping her get ready for the night. He kept the door of his bedchamber open enough so he would see the lady's maid when she walked down the hallway. It was ridiculous he was acting this way, of course. If one didn't know better, they would think he'd never been with a lady before.

But then, if he hadn't been with a lady, he wouldn't know what pleasures the bed offered a gentleman, and those pleasures were more intense when a lady showed enthusiasm for the activity. Fiona hadn't showed any enthusiasm with him. At least, she'd never shown any enthusiasm around him. When it came to the cook at his estate, however…

He shook his head. That was all in the past. The cook had been relieved of his duties long ago, and Fiona was cold in her grave. The only thing Grant had to remind him of that time was Lucinda, but one couldn't blame an innocent child for the way she was conceived. Everyone would believe Lucinda was really his. Since he was raising Lucinda, he would teach her how to be an honorable lady. Grant might not be Lucinda's father by flesh and blood, but he was still her father in every other sense of the word. In the end, that was what mattered.

Grant forced all of that from his mind. He didn't want to think of Fiona and how things were between them. None of it mattered anymore. He was just fortunate his second marriage wasn't anything like his first. This time, he had someone worth being with.

He heard a door shut from the other room. His gaze went to the hallway. The lady's maid passed by. Without thinking, he headed to the door separating his bedchamber from Carol's. He knocked on the door and waited for her to tell him to enter before he went into the room. She was just as beautiful as she'd been the previous evening, and again, she was only wearing the robe, a sign that let him know she was expecting him.

All day long, he'd been struggling to get rid of his erection. Finally, he didn't have to keep his thoughts off of this night. He drew her into his arms and kissed her. He kissed her on the lips, kissed her on the cheek, kissed her on the neck. As he kissed her, his hands traced the length of her body until they cupped her bottom. He pressed her intimately against him. Then he brought his lips back to hers and sought permission to enter her mouth. She parted her lips for him, and he interlaced his tongue with hers. His mind warned him to slow down, but ever since that morning, this was all he wanted to do. He was powerless to stop the passion sweeping through him.

Carol didn't seem to mind. She was kissing him in return, and she was squeezing his arms in a way that indicated she was excited to be with him. This was nice. Ideal even. There was nothing better than being with a lady who wanted to be with him.

He slid the robe off of her and then did the same with his robe. He took a good moment to look at her. She was even better naked. He leaned forward to kiss her again before he carried her to the bed. Last evening he'd had enough control to peel back the blankets before setting her on the bed, but he didn't have that kind of patience tonight. As soon as they were on the bed, he was kissing and touching her everywhere.

He told himself to slow down, that it would be wise to make sure she received her pleasure first, but that nagging part between his legs wasn't in the mood to wait any longer. If he didn't enter her—and enter her soon—he was going to climax outside of her body. Such a thing would be embarrassing. Whoever heard of a gentleman who lacked self-control like that?

He had to enter her. But he had to make sure she was ready for him. He reached down to the patch of curls between her legs and slid a finger into her. What a relief. She was already wet. He rolled on top of her and entered her. At once, the warmth of her flesh surrounded him. He moaned. She was still tight, but there was no barrier to push through. He didn't have to be as gentle with her as he'd been last night. He could give in to the need to relieve the sexual pressure that had been building up within him all day. He thrust inside her in earnest. The world around them faded away. All he was aware of was her. The way she had her legs wrapped around his waist. The way her hands held onto his arms. The way she groaned. Everything about this moment was perfect. There was no better source of pleasure a gentleman could ask for.

When he couldn't hold off on his release anymore, he cried out as his seed filled her core. He gasped. It was so intense. He had thought last night was the best climax he'd ever had, but this was even better. He tried to hold onto the moment for as long as possible, but it was gone much too soon. In its place, however, was the same feeling of contentment he'd had last night. This was something he could enjoy with her. It wasn't something he had to do out of necessity to have a child. When he was with Carol, he could really make love to her.

He relaxed and opened his eyes. At once, the world came flooding back around him. Carol was still holding him. She wasn't trying to roll away from him, as if the whole thing had bored her, as if she'd only done this because it was her duty. He lowered his head and kissed her in appreciation. She had no idea how nice it was that his experience with her was so different from what it'd been with Fiona.

Now that he didn't have his body pestering him for relief, he could focus on making sure she received her pleasure. He got off of her and brought his fingers between her legs. She lifted her hips to take him more fully into her. Then she moaned in the loveliest way. He really couldn't describe how beautiful it was to hear a lady voice her pleasure in bed, but it made him want to strive harder to bring her to completion.

He found her sensitive nub with his thumb and moved it in circular motions as his fingers stroked her core. Her moans grew louder. Her fingernails dug into his arms. Best of all, she rocked her hips in a way that made her breasts bounce. He especially liked that. He'd been looking at those breasts all day. He'd even taken the time to peer down her cleavage when he was certain no one noticed.

Yes, it had driven him to distraction with need. It was why he'd been so impatient to get her alone this evening. There was something about her breasts that fascinated him. And, watching her now, he felt his passion stirring once more. She grew still when she climaxed. He wanted the moment to last as long for her as possible, so he continued gently stroking her. When she was completely relaxed, she let out a contented sigh and turned toward him.

From there, they spent considerable time kissing each other. He had planned to go to sleep once he had satisfied her, but his erection notified him that he wasn't ready to stop for the night just yet. So, he rolled back on top of her and proceeded to make love to her again.

***

Carol read through the advertisement in the paper a second time. She'd heard of the Duchess of Ashbourne but hadn't ever considered using her services. Why would she? Her future had been arranged for her. She was supposed to marry the Duke of Augustine. Unlike her friends, she'd had no reason to attract suitors.

She tapped the edge of the paper and set it in her lap. She scanned the drawing room. At the moment, she was alone. Grant was out securing an investment. Amelia was getting ready for Reuben's visit. Lucinda was napping. That left her with a lot of time to think about how much her life had changed in a short time. What if that change could include a love match? Yes, Grant was happy with the marriage, but wouldn't securing his love be even better than simply being his companion?

Her gaze went back to the advertisement. She didn't think the duchess made it a habit of working with married ladies, but maybe she would consider it. Carol had some of her own money. She could pay her. If the duchess was placing an advertisement in the paper, that had to mean she needed clients. In such a case, she might not be particular about what kind of client she was getting.

Her gaze went to the desk where she spied parchment and the inkwell. Amelia wasn't due down here for another few minutes. That gave Carol enough time to write the Duchess of Ashbourne a missive.

Before she could talk herself out of it, she hurried over to the desk and retrieved a piece of parchment. Her heartbeat picked up as she sat down. She'd never done anything like this. For once in her life, she was making a decision without any prompting from another person. But this would be worth it if she managed to secure Grant's love.

She decided to make her petition to the duchess brief, figuring the less she said, the better. She had just sent out the missive when Amelia made her way to the drawing room.

"How do I look?" Amelia asked as she spun around in her peach gown.

"You look beautiful," Carol replied. "I notice that you're wearing your best jewelry for this afternoon's excursion."

"I thought since Reuben spent all of his childhood in the country, he might enjoy seeing the menagerie. I have to look my best if we'll be going out."

Carol grinned. "I don't know. I think the most interesting exhibit he'll find is you. Seems like an awful waste of money to have him discover that."

Amelia giggled. "When I first met you, I thought you were sweet, but I also thought you were a bit bland." She winced. "I don't mean that to be rude. I liked you. I thought you were going to be good for my brother and niece. But you're turning out to be a lot of fun. You're more passionate about things than you let on. I bet my brother likes that."

Carol hoped Amelia was right.

The butler stepped into the room with Reuben. Carol's eyes widened in surprise. She didn't think he was due to come here for another fifteen minutes.

"Forgive me for coming early," Reuben told Amelia. "I tried to wait but was too excited to make a couple more trips around the block."

To relieve Amelia from having to come up with a reply that wouldn't give away how eager she'd been to see Reuben, Carol said, "Your timing is perfect. We were just discussing how nice it would be to spend the day outside."

He glanced out the window. "It is nice out there. It'd be a shame to spend this visit indoors."

"Well, we will be indoors for some of it," Amelia replied. "Have you been to the menagerie yet?"

He shook his head. "I can't say I have. My brother doesn't think it's wise to be near dangerous animals."

Carol's eyebrows furrowed. Really? She didn't see how the exotic animals posed a threat when they were in cages.

"The workers at the menagerie make sure the visitors are safe," Amelia said. "You don't have anything to worry about. We even took my two-year-old niece there the other day, and she loved it."

"It was fun," Carol agreed. "But I suppose the menagerie isn't for everyone."

"I'd love to see it," Reuben said. "Because of you two, I won't have to go alone." He glanced at Amelia. "It's always more fun to do something when you have someone with you."

That would depend on who you were doing that something with. Carol managed to keep the thought to herself. It was obvious that these two were enamored with each other. She was certain if Grant was here, he would realize Reuben was going to propose. The only thing holding Reuben back right now was the fact that he didn't want to seem too eager.

She couldn't blame him for that. When it came to courting, she'd noticed that those who didn't seem eager ended up securing marriages a lot sooner than those who were eager. There seemed to be a delicate balance when it came to love. With any luck, she might be able to find that balance in her own marriage.

Chapter Twelve

"I've never had a married lady contact me before," the Duchess of Ashbourne told Carol a few days later as Carol stepped into the duchess' drawing room. She gestured for Carol to sit then instructed the butler to bring in some tea and crumpets. After he left, she went to join Carol at the settee. "I must admit that I'm intrigued. Why would you want my assistance?"

Carol took a deep breath to calm her pounding heart. It was easy to see why so many people were in awe of the duchess. The lady had a way of exuding confidence that so many, including Carol, lacked. Carol offered a smile. "I want my husband to fall in love with me." Noting the surprise on the duchess' face, she added, "It sounds pathetic, doesn't it?"

"No, it's not pathetic at all. In fact, it's a sensible request."

"Is it?"

The lady nodded. "Things go much better in a marriage when you secure the love of your husband." She paused then lowered her voice. "I can't help you if he already loves someone else."

"He doesn't. I don't think he even loved his first wife." She shrugged. "He didn't tell me anything about her, but from what his sister said, it sounds like the marriage wasn't that good. I'd like it to be different with me. I think he's the most wonderful gentleman I've ever come across. I suspect I might already love him, even if we only recently married."

"It's good you care for him so deeply, but are you absolutely sure he has no one else? A mistress, perhaps?"

"No, he has no mistress." Carol couldn't tell her how she knew this. She might not have a lot of experience making love, but he was far too anxious when he came to her bed for her to think he was taking care of his needs with another lady. That was something she liked. She'd rather he meet those needs with her than someone else.

"All right," the duchess said. "You've convinced me that there is no one you are competing with for his affections. Things are a lot simpler when it's just you and him."

Carol nodded but held back on saying more since the butler came into the room with a tray full of refreshments.

The duchess instructed the butler to close the door on his way out. After he did, she gave Carol her full attention. "Since we'll be working together, we might as well get better acquainted. It'll help us be more comfortable with each other. Being comfortable helps to make the lessons go more smoothly. I'm Helena."

"I'm Carol."

"All right, Carol. I need to figure out the best way to start. Typically, a lady is entering her first Season, so she doesn't know who she'll end up marrying. Since this situation is different, I should approach this as if you finally found a gentleman you'd like to encourage to be your suitor. This is the stage where she isn't certain if he likes her. I can teach you how to flirt."

"Flirt?"

"You said he's agreeable about the marriage, but he hasn't come out and told you he loves you. Sometimes gentlemen can be shy about expressing their feelings. Flirting gives them the nudge they need."

"Gentlemen are shy about expressing their feelings?" Carol blurted out in surprise.

"Some are."

Really? Carol wouldn't have guessed that. "I assumed gentlemen have no trouble expressing their feelings since all of them seem so confident."

"It's easy to think that when we are the ones who have to wait for them to initiate the relationship. Did your husband propose to you, or was your marriage arranged?"

"He proposed. He didn't know me at the time, though. A common friend suggested we would make a good match. I suppose it was an arrangement of sorts."

"This common friend must be a good one in order for both of you to take such a big risk."

Carol nodded. "I'd say this friend is a good judge of character."

"Given how much you adore your husband, I'd have to agree." Helena picked up a cup of tea and gave it to her. Then she picked up her own cup. "Even though gentlemen are expected to take the lead, our role as ladies doesn't have to be a passive one. If we like a certain gentleman and suspect he likes us, we can do our part to prompt things along. That's what flirting does. It's our way of telling the gentlemen that we love them without coming out and actually saying it."

"I wouldn't mind telling Grant I love him if he would tell me he loves me first. I don't want to embarrass myself by saying the words in case he doesn't feel the same way."

"You deserve to know he loves you before committing all of yourself to him," Helena assured her then took a sip of her tea.

Carol relaxed and sipped her own tea. It was nice that Helena understood her. She didn't have to feel so awkward anymore. Or inadequate.

Helena put her cup down. "We'll start with the easiest way you can flirt. If you're not near him, you can glance his way, and if he happens to look at you, give him a slight smile. If you smile and he doesn't look away, you can twirl your hair around your finger or brush your hair gently away from your face. Then you can turn your attention back to whatever you were doing before you glanced his way. You don't want to look at him too long. A couple of seconds is all you need. I'll show you what I mean."

Carol watched as the duchess went to the window. The duchess peered outside for a moment then glanced at Carol. She proceeded to give Carol a hint of a smile before she brushed her fingers against the strand of curls that framed her face. Then she turned her gaze back to the window.

Carol took a deep breath and released it. That seemed simple enough. She could do something like that.

Helena returned to her. "If you happen to be talking to him, you can do more things. An easy thing to do is to laugh when he says something witty. Even if he's not very good at telling jokes, you'll want to laugh. It'll boost his confidence. If he's trying to make you laugh, then he's putting forth effort into pleasing you. By laughing, you're letting him know it's working."

Carol hadn't known Grant for long, but he didn't seem like the type who told jokes. He seemed like he was more of a serious gentleman. But that was the point, wasn't it? If he did tell her a joke, then it would prove he was interested enough in her to try to please her.

"Also," Helena began as she picked up a crumpet, "a compliment goes a long way. Every gentleman will have some trait that makes him attractive. Mention it during the conversation."

"How should I do that?"

"Let's say he happens to have a good sense of humor, and you truly do enjoy his jokes. After he tells a couple of them, you can say, 'You're so witty.' Let's say he is more considerate than funny. In that case, you can say, 'Your consideration of other people is commendable.'"

That was just as easy to do as the smile and thing with the hair. So far, the tips the duchess was giving her on flirting were perfectly doable.

"Sometimes gentlemen respond better to touch than to words," Helena began. "Next time you're close to him, touch his arm. If you weren't married, I'd say make the action quick, but since you are married, you can let your hand rest on his arm if you want. While touching him, you can offer him a compliment. It's like this." The duchess laughed and touched Carol's arm. "I had no idea you had such a marvelous sense of humor, my lord." Then she pulled her hand away. "If he responds well to that, you can tilt your head slightly to the side and twirl your hair around your finger or flutter your eyelashes at him."

"How do I flutter my eyelashes?"

Helena demonstrated how to do it.

Carol repeated the action, but it felt a bit awkward.

She chuckled. "Don't move your eyelashes so fast. Slow it down a bit. He'll think there's something in your eyes otherwise."

Oh. Despite a surge of embarrassment, Carol renewed her efforts and gave her eyelashes another flutter.

"That was good," Helena encouraged, "but next time try to smile while you're doing it."

Carol tried it but found the smile faltering since she was concentrating on fluttering her eyelashes. "That's surprisingly difficult to do at the same time."

"I know, but if you practice, it'll come more easily. It'll even help if you do this in front of a mirror so you can see how you look while you're doing it. I assure you that it won't seem awkward once you get used to it. Flirting is a skill. The more you do it, the more natural it is."

"And it'll make my husband fall in love with me?"

"I think your husband will be flattered when you flirt with him. I can't come out and guarantee he will fall in love with you, but I can say that the things you are doing could lead to love."

In that case, Carol would be sure to follow Helena's tips on flirting.

In a lower voice, Helena said, "I haven't recommended this to any of my previous clients since they weren't married yet, but since you are, I could make some suggestions on things you can do to encourage him to take you to his bed."

Carol's face warmed. Did married ladies do such a thing? She thought they were supposed to wait for their husbands to initiate lovemaking.

"I can't speak for other ladies," Helena continued, "but as someone who is fortunate to have a husband who loves her very much, it's rather nice when I know I can convince my husband to drop everything he's doing to take me to bed. Part of romantic love is intimacy. And…it's rather fun to see if you can coax your husband to make love during the day."

People didn't have to wait until it was night before going to bed together? She bit her lower lip. There were times during the day when she wanted to be with Grant. Why, just yesterday, she'd been reflecting on the new position she and Grant had done the previous night in bed. She'd had a terrible time reading her book because of the built-up tension between her legs. Grant hadn't been the only one who'd been anxious with need as soon as it was time for bed last night. She'd already been wet by the time he finally came to her. There had been that hour when Amelia had taken Lucinda out, and she and Grant had played cards. It would have been much more fun being in bed than playing a card game.

Carol cleared her throat. "What do you do when you want to encourage your husband to take you to bed?"

"I'm glad you asked because this part of flirting is a lot more fun." With a grin, the duchess proceeded to teach her everything she knew on the topic.

Chapter Thirteen

"Carol isn't with you?" Grant asked Amelia after she arrived home.

Amelia placed the new hat and gloves she'd purchased on the dresser in her bedchamber. "I can't believe you followed me all the way upstairs to ask me about Carol."

He lowered his gaze so she wouldn't pick up on his uncertainty. He should have just waited for her to go to the drawing room. He shouldn't have headed up here as soon as he saw her come home. After being with Fiona, he should have a stronger mask to hide his insecurities. It was just that he'd gone visit Horatio when Amelia and Carol left, and he knew that Carol wasn't visiting Rachel because Rachel was at Horatio's. Also, Lydia hadn't returned to London yet, so she couldn't be visiting her other friend. Amelia was the only person he thought Carol would spend the afternoon with.

"Maybe Carol went out to get a hat or gloves like I did," Amelia suggested.

So as not to seem weak, he nodded. "Yes, she probably went shopping." Though, if Carol was going to do that, why didn't she just go with Amelia? Amelia had told him and Carol that she was going to the market while they were eating breakfast.

"I'm sure there's nothing to worry about," Amelia said as she headed for the door. "She won't get lost in the market."

He forced himself to smile at her joke. Deciding to joke in return, he said, "I'd feel better if she had taken Lucinda along. Lucinda can always find her way back here. It's where her toy horse is."

Amelia laughed. "I had no idea when I picked that thing up, she'd develop such an attachment to it. I think it's rather sweet. Speaking of Lucinda, isn't it time for her to get up from her nap?"

"The maid will wake her in a few more minutes."

"We should have some tea and a crumpet ready for her when she brings her down. I know I get cranky if I don't get my treat when I'm hungry."

He smiled, again, at her attempt to brighten his mood. He hoped she wasn't teasing him because she picked up on his apprehension. He hoped she was only doing it because she was in a joking mood.

Grant followed Amelia down to the drawing room and sat in a chair while she asked the butler to bring in refreshments. He hated feeling insecure. The first couple of times Fiona had run off without telling him where she was going, he didn't think anything of it. He'd just assumed she'd been shopping or visiting friends.

The thought of adultery never crossed his mind. It wasn't until a friend suggested he be careful in case she had another gentleman's child that he started to watch her. And when he did, it confirmed that the acquaintance had good reason to warn him. He really liked Carol. In fact, there were moments he suspected he was even falling in love with her. He didn't know what he'd do if he found out she took a lover.

"I hope Reuben will be at the ball tonight," Amelia said. "He doesn't go to all of them. I'd hate to think that I'll pretty myself up for nothing."

Grant forced his attention to his sister. "Even if he's not there, you should enjoy yourself. There's no point in sulking about it."

"I won't sulk. I'll just wish he was there, that's all."

He wasn't sure how she could enjoy the ball if she was going to dwell on Reuben all evening.

The butler brought in the tray, and soon, the maid brought Lucinda down. Grant tried not to peek at the clock, but he did anyway. An hour had passed since he returned home, and Carol still wasn't there. Ignoring the knot in his stomach, he picked up a crumpet and bit into it.

"Lucinda, I was thinking that we should go to Hyde Park," Amelia said as she brought Lucinda onto her lap. "If your father is inclined, maybe we can even go for a hot air balloon ride." She turned a hopeful gaze in Grant's direction. "What do you think? I heard they're a lot of fun."

Grant glanced at the doorway. He needed to focus on his sister and his daughter. "It sounds dangerous."

"It isn't dangerous. People do it all the time."

"But you're all the way up in the air. It's not natural."

Amelia giggled. "That's what makes it fun. We can be up in the air like the birds. It'll be like flying."

"Want fly!" Lucinda said in excitement.

"I love how she isn't afraid to say what she wants," Amelia mused. "It's so nice, isn't it?"

"I suppose it's all right for a child, but I hope she learns to watch her tongue when she's an adult," Grant replied.

"She'll learn to watch what she says as she gets older," Amelia assured him. "We all do."

Grant relaxed. Amelia was probably right. He probably worried too much about the kind of lady Lucinda would turn out to be. His gaze went back to the doorway. This time, he wasn't left unsatisfied. Carol was stepping into the room.

His first reaction was relief. Then his apprehension returned. She didn't have any items with her that would indicate she'd been shopping. So what had she been doing? Did she look like a lady who had just met her lover? It was impossible to tell.

Amelia waved Carol over. "You're just in time. We were talking about going for a hot air balloon ride."

"I don't know," Carol slowly replied as she walked over to them. "I've seen them, and they look dangerous."

Carol sat in the chair next to Grant. That was promising, wasn't it? She wouldn't want to sit near him if she'd been unfaithful to him. She looked over at him and smiled. At once, he relaxed. Fiona could never make eye contact with him after one of her dalliances.

"You two are so much alike it's frightening," Amelia said. "Would you believe Grant was just saying the same thing?"

"Well, I see no reason why anyone would want to be all the way up in the air," Grant commented. "What do you accomplish?"

"You have fun," Amelia replied. "And sometimes having fun is enough of a reason to do something." Her gaze went to Carol. "Who cares if you're only going to go up into the air and come right back down? It'll be fun to see London from way up high."

Carol's smile faltered a bit, an indication that she was growing uncomfortable. "Maybe it's fun, but it also sounds scary. What if something goes wrong? What if the balloon doesn't stay up in the air like it's supposed to? What if it pops?"

"I agree with her," Grant told his sister. "I heard of a hot air balloon that did fall too fast from the sky. A couple of people got hurt."

"Yes, but that rarely happens, and the owner made sure the balloon was repaired," Amelia protested. "Most of the time, nothing bad ever happens. You can't let fear hold you back from having fun."

"Want fly," Lucinda piped up. "Want fun."

Amelia gave Grant an imploring look. He shook his head. Maybe it made him dull, but he had no desire to go up in a hot air balloon ride.

"Well, can I take Lucinda?" Amelia asked.

Noting the excitement on Lucinda's face, Grant figured he could relent in this area. Amelia was probably right. Nothing bad was going to happen. He was sure the two would come home and tell him that he and Carol worried for nothing. Besides, it would allow him time alone with Carol.

"You can take her," Grant replied.

"Oh, good!" Holding Lucinda, Amelia jumped to her feet. "We better go before he changes his mind," she told Lucinda. To Grant and Carol, she said, "You two will miss a fun adventure. I look forward to telling you all about it."

"We look forward to hearing it," Grant replied, still not persuaded that the hot air balloon trip was worth going on. He waited until Amelia and Lucinda were out of the room before he turned his attention back to Carol. "Thankfully, she's not the type to gloat for too long. We won't hear any more about how we missed out on a fun afternoon once today is over."

"Maybe she thinks it'll be fun, but I don't see the appeal in it. I would rather be here."

His heart leapt. Did she mean she'd rather be with him? He waited for a long moment before asking, "Did you have a good time out?"

"I did. It was an interesting afternoon." Before he could ask where she went, she added, "What about you? Did you have a good visit with Horatio?"

He frowned. Was she sincerely interested in how things went with Horatio, or was she trying to get him distracted so he wouldn't ask her more about her afternoon?

"Forgive me," she said. "It's not my business to know what gentlemen do. I need to remember my place." She took a sip of tea.

His frown deepened, but this time for a different reason. Why would she think she had no right to know anything about what he did with his time? Did her guardian put that idea into her head?

"There's nothing wrong with asking me about my day," he said after choosing the best way to respond. "Just as there's nothing wrong with me asking you about your day. We're married. It'd be nice if we took an interest in each other's lives, wouldn't it?"

Her face lit up with such pleasure that he was assured he had said the right thing. He relaxed. She hadn't shut him out like Fiona had.

"It would be nice," she said.

Figuring it was up to him to take the lead, he ventured, "I had an enjoyable time today. Horatio introduced me to Lord Steinbeck and Mr. Jasper. The investment they're interested in sounds promising. I think it'll yield good results in the years to come."

"I'm glad. I've only heard about Lord Steinbeck and Mr. Jasper. My uncle envies their ability to make money."

"If you'd like, I could see if they would be willing to meet your uncle."

She balked, and right away, he knew she didn't want to have anything to do with her uncle.

"Forgive me. I was only trying to help. I didn't mean to make you uncomfortable," he said. "I suppose not every niece likes her uncle."

"Of course, I like my uncle. He's a part of my family." She averted her gaze from him and sipped more tea.

She reminded him so much of himself in the way she said that. That was the exact same tone and those were the exact same words he had used when speaking about Fiona whenever someone asked him if he liked her. He hesitated to respond. They were having a pleasant conversation, and she had chosen to stay here with him rather than go for a hot air balloon ride. It would be a shame to ruin this afternoon by treading into unpleasant territory.

Carol set her cup down, and his gaze instinctively went to her breasts. She had very nice breasts. They were large enough to fill her gown while also giving him a good view of her cleavage whenever she leaned forward. She sat back up. For a moment, he was disappointed. But then she twirled a few strands of hair around her fingers and let her hand fall to the top of her cleavage. He made eye contact with her, and she gave him a smile that invited him to kiss her.

She didn't need to prompt him further. The surge of warmth flooding his loins made him act on his baser desires. He took her in his arms and brought his mouth to hers. She wrapped her arms around his shoulders and invited him to deepen the kiss, which he was more than happy to do. Few things in the world were as wonderful as a lady who wanted to be kissed.

He had only intended for the kissing to go on for a short while, but the more time they spent kissing, the more his body urged him to find satisfaction before evening. Amelia and Lucinda were out. He and Carol didn't have anywhere to go until the ball, and it was still a good three hours before they had to get ready for the event. There was plenty of time to enjoy things of a more intimate nature. Why spend time in torment if he didn't have to? Carol was letting him know she was willing to make love to him right now. Decision made, he ended the kiss, took her hand, and led her to his bed.

***

Carol rested in Grant's arms after he made love to her. She shouldn't be surprised, and yet, she was. Helena had a reputation for helping people fall in love. It was why Carol had sought her services. But she hadn't expected the duchess' advice to work so quickly…and so well. If a sequence of actions like leaning forward, touching her hair, and then letting her hand fall right above her breasts could prompt Grant to initiate lovemaking, then Carol had no doubt that the other flirting tricks Helena taught her would make Grant fall in love with her.

Carol was so excited that she couldn't doze off to sleep like Grant had. There was a lot to do before the ball. She had to bathe. She had to pick out the perfect gown for the evening to complement the rosy color in her cheeks. She needed the lady's maid's help in styling her hair. Then she had to practice the things Helena had taught her. With a glance at her sleeping husband, Carol kissed his cheek then got out of bed.

Chapter Fourteen

"I can't recall a time I've seen you as happy as you are right now," Rachel told Carol as the two friends stood at the side of the room of Lord Whitney's ball. "This marriage is good for you."

"It has been good for me." Carol's gaze went to her husband, and her heartbeat picked up.

At the moment, he was talking to Horatio, Lord Steinbeck, and Mr. Jasper near the refreshments. The four seemed to be getting along well. Unlike the Duke of Augustine, Grant didn't have that horrible scowl on his face. No. He was smiling and laughing. She'd like to think that part of his happiness stemmed from being with her.

Grant glanced in her direction, so she offered him a smile. He returned the smile. Heartbeat picking up, she decided to brush a curl back from her face before turning her attention back to Rachel so that she could finish the flirtatious gesture Helena had taught her.

"Don't tell Grant this," Rachel spoke up, "but Horatio has a lot of respect for him. He has a reputation for conducting himself well in every situation. Many gentlemen look up to him."

"Do they?"

Rachel nodded. "He's a good gentleman. I think you two are an ideal match. What a relief it is that you married him instead of the Duke of Augustine."

"Grant is wonderful. I didn't think it was possible to love someone so soon. I always thought love was supposed to take a year or longer to develop. Now, I know differently."

"I'm happy for you, Carol."

Realizing they were only talking about her and Grant, Carol hurried to ask, "How are things with Edwin? How is he adjusting to life now that he's not a butler?"

"Edwin is managing fine." Rachel chuckled. "He has to stop himself from doing some of the things the new butler does. He says it comes out of habit."

"I suppose it would be difficult to stop doing something when you're used to doing it all the time." She scanned the room. "Where is he?"

"He is speaking with Mr. St. George and Lord Crampton. They're younger than the gentlemen Horatio is talking to, and I think that makes him more comfortable."

Rachel gestured to the corner of the room, and Carol's gaze finally settled on Edwin. Edwin was a bit stiff, but he was holding up his end of the conversation while talking to the two gentlemen. "I can't imagine how difficult it would be to go from being a servant to being a member of London's wealthy elite, but he seems to be doing a good job of it. You can barely tell he's nervous."

"He does a marvelous job of hiding his apprehension. Maybe he had to learn to do that while working for my family. I'm sure being a servant can't be easy. They're expected to do so much for us, and sometimes we aren't all that pleasant."

Carol shook her head but smiled. "Rachel, you and your family are among the nicest people in London. I doubt working in your household was a burden."

If Edwin had worked in her uncle's household, things would have been difficult. Her uncle hadn't just been mean to her; he'd been mean to the servants as well. There were times when he would yell at them for not doing things exactly the way he wanted them to be done. Just thinking about it made her glad she was no longer living in his townhouse.

"I wonder how long Lydia plans to stay away from London," Rachel said after a long moment.

"If Lord Quinton is as bad as everyone makes him sound, then maybe she never plans to return," Carol replied.

"Oh, he doesn't embarrass her at all. She's quick to defend him. I think she'd be proud to be seen with him."

Really? Carol considered the kind of person Lydia was. She supposed between the three of them, Lydia was the one who overlooked people's flaws the most. She did have those two brothers. While Felix and Oscar were nice, they had a tendency to be annoying. Felix was stuffy and impatient, and Oscar liked to hide pieces of food in his clothes so he could nibble on something when he thought no one was looking. In light of all that, Carol shouldn't be surprised Lydia had taken a liking to someone as strange as Lord Quinton. Maybe someone normal would have bored her. She recalled how disinterested Lydia had been whenever Rachel offered to speak with Horatio about marrying her.

"I always wondered about something," Carol began. "Did you ever ask Horatio if he would marry Lydia to help her family out?"

"Several times. He never liked the idea. He thinks of Lydia like a sister." She shrugged. "I did my best. I thought they'd make a good match. But who knows? Maybe she'll be happier with Lord Quinton."

"And maybe Horatio will find someone who'll interest him in a more romantic way," Carol agreed. "Maybe Lord Quinton came to the right dinner party at the right time."

Rachel thought over Carol's comment for a moment and nodded. "Perhaps he did."

"Pardon me," a gentleman spoke up.

At first, Carol thought the gentleman was Grant, but a quick glance in the direction where Grant was still talking with the gentlemen dimmed that spark of excitement. She was still allowed to have one more dance with him, and she was greatly anticipating it. Instead of Grant, the person standing before her was the gentleman from the menagerie who had told her and Grant about zebra stripes.

When she realized he was focused on her, rather than Rachel, she knew she had to be the one who answered. "May I help you, Mr. Weber?"

"I only came over to ask if you enjoyed your visit to the menagerie," he said.

Carol glanced at her friend. There was something deeply troubling about the gentleman. Having her friend near helped to calm her nerves. Carol forced a smile and told Rachel, "My husband and I went to the menagerie, and Mr. Weber explained that no two zebras have the same pattern of stripes."

"Oh really?" Rachel's eyebrows rose in interest. "I didn't know that."

"They are quite fascinating creatures," Mr. Weber said. "They're social animals. They like to live in groups. If one gets injured and is cornered by an attacker, they will come together to protect the injured."

Since he glanced between them expectantly, Carol offered the only reply she could think of. "I didn't know that. Did you know that, Rachel?"

Rachel shook her head. "To be honest, I don't know anything about zebras except that they have black and white stripes."

"Yes," Mr. Weber began, "and from a distance, you'll think they are all the same. It's not until you get a closer look that you realize how different each one is."

Carol didn't know why he directed that comment to her when Rachel was the one who had talked to him. She shifted uncomfortably from one foot to the other. She couldn't be sure, but it seemed like he had taken an interest in her, and she wasn't certain it was the good kind of interest. Not that she would desire a good kind of interest from him. The only gentleman she wanted was Grant, and things were looking particularly promising with him. Her gaze went to Grant. Her face flushed when she realized he was looking in her direction.

"Zebras can be found in a variety of places," Mr. Weber continued to say, keeping his focus on her. "Africa is a diverse continent. It has grasslands, deserts, and mountains. It's quite an experience to visit there."

Carol reluctantly turned her gaze back to him. Why was he telling her all of this? Hadn't he heard Grant address her as Lady Wright? She cleared her throat. "Um, yes, I'm sure Africa is a lovely place to visit."

Mr. Weber chuckled. "It's more than a place. It contains many countries. Perhaps you've heard of Egypt?"

Why was he only directing his comments to her? Carol shot her friend a pleading look.

"Yes, of course, we've heard of Egypt," Rachel inserted. "Why, it wasn't all that long ago I was talking with someone who'd been there. He said the pyramids are awe-inspiring."

He gave a brief look in Rachel's direction. "Yes, they are impressive." His gaze returned to Carol. "But that's just one country in Africa. Further south is where you'll find the exotic animals you enjoyed viewing in the menagerie."

Carol didn't like the way he kept directing his attention to her. He didn't look at her the same way Grant did. When Grant looked at her, there was a tenderness in his eyes. When Mr. Weber looked at her, it seemed as if he was trying to find something wrong with her. But why? She didn't know him. What could she have done to warrant such disfavor?

"Why don't we share the next dance?" he suggested. "Then I can tell you more about Africa, and you can tell me something interesting that you've experienced."

There was no way she was going to dance with him, even if it was impolite to decline the offer.

Before she could answer, a familiar voice said, "Mr. Weber, I'd like to have a moment of your time."

Her gaze went to Grant, and she breathed a sigh of relief. Good. Now she was spared from having to be rude to Mr. Weber.

"I certainly don't mind talking with you, my lord," Mr. Weber said. "Perhaps we may do so after the dance? It's just about to get started."

Carol felt a flicker of panic rise up within her, but Grant stepped in front of her. "Considering the fact that I am the lady's husband, we will talk now."

Mr. Weber hesitated to respond then smiled. "Since you put it that way, I'll be delighted to speak with you now. I suppose you want to do this in private?"

Without returning the gentleman's smile, Grant nodded. "This way, please." Grant waved to another side of the room.

Carol waited for Grant to look over at her so she could let him know she was glad he had intervened on her behalf, but he didn't glance in her direction as he left with Mr. Weber.

Rachel frowned. "I wonder what all that was about."

Carol turned her attention back to her friend. "I have no idea why Mr. Weber wanted to speak about Africa or animals. I don't even know him. He happened to be at the menagerie when Grant and I went there with Lucinda. He came up to us and started talking."

"Do you think he wants to have an affair with you?" Rachel whispered.

Carol gasped. "No. It seems more like he's accusing me of something, but I have no idea what that is." She shivered. "In some ways, he reminds me of the Duke of Augustine."

"That's not the impression I got. It almost seems like he's your lover."

"But he's not. I only want to be with Grant."

"I know you do. Everyone can tell how much you adore him by the way you look at him."

"Can Grant tell that?" Carol asked.

"I can't tell, but it's rather sweet he swooped in to stop Mr. Weber from taking you to the dance floor. Edwin said that when Lord Swenson came over for a visit, he had to fight back his jealousy. He was jealous because he loved me and didn't want to see me with someone else. Grant just exhibited how jealous he is of you. Edwin was only a butler at the time, so he couldn't step in to stop Lord Swenson from talking to me, but, as someone who isn't a servant, Grant could stop Mr. Weber." Rachel gave her a wink. "I think that's telling."

Carol's ears perked up in interest. "You think Grant may already love me?"

"If he doesn't already, he will soon."

Really? Carol searched for Grant but couldn't find him in the crowded room. What a shame. She wished she could have more than two dances with him at these balls. If it was up to her, she'd have every dance with him. But they were married, so she shared the townhouse with him. Better than that, they shared a bed. When they were home, she'd get to be in his arms. She couldn't wait.

Chapter Fifteen

"Lady Wright is married," Grant told Mr. Weber from the corner of the room. He had picked a place that was as far from Carol as they could get. The more distance he put between Mr. Weber and Carol, the better. He would have thrown Mr. Weber out of the townhouse, but he didn't own the place. "You will not dance with her. You will not talk to her. As far as you are concerned, she doesn't exist."

Mr. Weber laughed. "From the way you're acting, one would swear I was having a dalliance with her. I only asked her to dance, and I was only talking to her about Africa. You can ask her. Ask that friend of hers, too, if you don't believe me."

Grant scowled. "I'm not a fool, Mr. Weber. I know when a gentleman is showing more interest in a married lady than he should." He might not have known it when Fiona was alive, but he knew it now. "Lady Wright is not for you. She is my wife. You need to direct your attention to the single ladies at this ball."

Mr. Weber put his hand over his heart. "I assure you that my interest in her is not the least bit romantic."

"Don't lie to me."

"I'm not lying. I'm telling you the truth. My intentions are honorable."

"Oh? Then what are your intentions?"

The gentleman paused for a moment then said, "I can't say yet. Too much is at stake."

Grant narrowed his eyes at him. What exactly did he mean by that? "I don't know what you're trying to prove, but I won't tolerate you getting near my wife again."

Grant stared at Mr. Weber, willing him to back down. Mr. Weber wasn't one of his servants, so he didn't look away from him as Grant had hoped he would. The cook had known better than to fight back. He had left the estate in disgrace. Mr. Weber, however, seemed to believe he had every right to get close to a married lady. And that frightened Grant. But he was determined not to show it.

Finally, Mr. Weber shrugged. "I can't disclose everything to you right now. I only hope when I can, I'll find that you aren't complicit in a crime."

"What crime? I'm not the one seeking an adulterous affair."

"That's not what I mean, but I understand that's what you think."

Grant didn't like the game Mr. Weber was playing with him, and he was about to let him know it when Mr. Weber walked away. Grant watched him. Fortunately, he didn't go back to Carol. Instead, he left the ballroom. Grant clenched his jaw. If he wasn't a gentleman, he would run after Mr. Weber and punch him until he agreed to leave Carol alone. But he was a gentleman, and because he was a gentleman, he had to restrain his baser emotions.

Grant glanced at the people nearby to make sure no one was watching him before he sat in a chair. He had to calm down. He was so upset he was shaking. When he found out Fiona had gotten pregnant while he was in London, he had her locked in her bedchamber until she told him who the father of the child was. Ironically, he had sent Fiona to the estate in order to prevent her from having another gentleman's child. A lot of good that did him.

He didn't want to send Carol to his estate. He had things he needed to do in London, and he wanted to spend time with her. Mr. Weber was expressing an interest in her, but that didn't make her guilty. It was possible the chance encounter at the menagerie hadn't been a chance after all. He felt sick to his stomach. Maybe the two knew each other before that day. Maybe she'd agreed to marry him because she was already with child and hoped to hide her indiscretion.

No, that wasn't right. She'd been a virgin on their wedding night. He had to push through her maidenhead. The pain in his stomach eased. There was no reason to suspect that Carol had known Mr. Weber before that day at the menagerie. But Carol had been gone for some time earlier today, and he wasn't sure what she'd been doing. It was possible she'd met up with Mr. Weber. It was also possible she hadn't met up with him at all. It was possible she was innocent of any wrongdoing.

He didn't know how to proceed from here. Should he come out and ask her about it? If he did, could he believe what she said? Sometimes it was hard to detect the truth, and he knew his fears would get in the way of thinking clearly. He could ask his sister for help, but he didn't think it was wise to get Amelia involved. If he did, he'd have to explain what happened with Fiona, and he didn't want to do that. He wanted Amelia to think Lucinda was his child. He wanted Carol to think Lucinda was his child. It was important the girl have a life free from the stigma of illegitimacy. He wanted Lucinda to marry a respectable gentleman and have a good life. He also wanted his second marriage to be better than his first.

He waited until he was no longer shaking before he stood up. He took a deep breath and released it. He could not assume Carol was having an affair. He could not assume she was even interested in having an affair. He could not assume that even if Mr. Weber wanted to be her lover that she wanted the same. Things were going well so far in this marriage. The last thing he wanted to do was jeopardize that. Fiona's sins were Fiona's sins. Not all ladies were unfaithful to their husbands. He needed to be fair to Carol.

With that in mind, he made his way over to the side of the room where he had left her. She was still talking with her friend, but Horatio and Edwin had joined them. That helped to set his mind at ease. He could trust Horatio not to betray him. Edwin was obviously in love with Rachel. Someone would have to be blind not to notice his devotion to her.

Grant couldn't help but wonder if others could detect his feelings for Carol. Perhaps Mr. Weber had noticed and thought it was amusing to pursue her. Maybe he was one of those gentlemen who liked to steal ladies from their husbands. Grant shook the thought off. He needed to remain calm if he was to think clearly.

"We were beginning to think you disappeared," Horatio joked when they noticed Grant approach. "Poor Carol was going to have to walk home tonight."

Rachel swatted her brother's arm. "Don't say things like that." With a look at Grant, she said, "We knew you didn't abandon Carol at this ball. Horatio thinks he's funny."

Grant smiled. "I know he was joking." His gaze went to Carol. "I think it's almost time for the next dance. I don't suppose you'd be interested in having the second one allotted to us?"

A pleasant shade of pink graced Carol's cheeks, and he hoped it was his offer that was responsible for the blush. "I'd love to dance," she replied.

"In that case, this might be a good time for us to dance, too," Edwin told Rachel.

"It's just my luck there's not another lady here to dance with," Horatio said in amusement. "I feel like an unaccompanied animal on Noah's Ark."

"You could have a dancing partner if you had married Lydia when I suggested it," Rachel pointed out. "Now, you'll have to find a lady on your own." She slipped her arm around Edwin's and let him escort her to the dance floor.

"She never lets me forget that I refused to marry Lydia," Horatio said with a wry grin. "I realize some gentlemen would balk at how my sister talks to me, but I like that she speaks her mind. I'd rather have the honesty."

"Honesty is important, no matter what the relationship is like," Grant agreed with a glance at Carol. It was impossible to tell if she agreed with him or not. She didn't nod, but she didn't give a slight roll of her eyes like Fiona would have done, either.

"Enjoy your dance," Horatio told Grant and Carol before he headed for a group of gentlemen.

Grant glanced around the room to make sure Mr. Weber was still gone. As much as he wanted to ask her about this afternoon, he had to bide his time and wait until they were alone. The last thing he wanted to do was let her know he suspected her of inappropriate behavior. If she turned out to be innocent, it would hurt the foundation they were building. Putting on a smile to make those around them think that all was right, he led her to the dancing area.

***

Grant held Carol in his arms after they made love. He'd thought once they arrived at the townhouse, he would find a subtle way to ask her about her afternoon, but the words failed him. How did one approach a topic when they worried they wouldn't hear the answer they wanted? Carol had been incredibly sweet after the second dance. She'd been attentive to everything he'd said. She'd lean toward him in a way that let him know he wasn't boring her. Sometimes she had even touched him, and even if the touch was brief, it stirred his passions and made him want to do more than talk about the afternoon.

Fiona had never shown an interest in him. Certainly, the fact that Carol showed an interest had to mean that she wasn't considering an affair with Mr. Weber. He knew he couldn't play the part of the doting husband if he was seeing a mistress. His guilt would get the best of him. He closed his eyes. It was irritating that Fiona kept getting in his way. He didn't want to think about her. He'd thought the memory of her died the day he buried her. He hadn't realized marrying again would dig up her memory from the grave. What would it take to be free of her?

Carol lifted her head from his shoulder. "Is something wrong?"

He opened his eyes and saw the concerned expression on her face as she peered down at him. How did she know something was wrong? He hadn't said anything, and he'd been careful not to sigh. Amelia had warned him that people could tell something bothered him when he sighed.

He weighed his words before he spoke. "It occurred to me that we didn't really talk about our afternoons." Yes, that was a good way to introduce this difficult topic. "If we are going to be companions, in addition to being husband and wife, we ought to be able to speak freely about what we do when we're not together. As you know, I went to visit Horatio. Lord Steinbeck and Mr. Jasper had told us about a rail line connecting Manchester and Liverpool. It's due to open later this year. The rail line will run only on steam power, and it'll run passengers as well as goods. Lord Steinbeck and Mr. Jasper think it'll be a boon to both Manchester and Liverpool. Today, Horatio and I gave them some money to invest in it." He paused when he sensed her mind had started to wander. "Am I boring you?"

She flushed and gave a light chuckle. "I've heard of rail lines, but I don't know enough about them. I also have no idea what steam power is."

"Do you want me to explain more about these things to you?"

"Is this something that interests you a lot?"

"No, not really. I'm just excited by the prospect this will yield a financial benefit." Without meaning to, she had given him the opportunity to discuss what he was really interested in. "Why don't we talk about your afternoon? Where did you go?"

She hesitated for several moments before saying, "I went out for a walk. The day was such a nice one. I didn't want to waste it."

She hadn't answered him right away. That wasn't good. He cleared his throat. "I noticed Amelia was here when I got home. I'm sure she would have enjoyed taking that walk with you."

"Oh, well, I think she would be more interested in responding to the correspondence Reuben sent than she would be in a walk. Reuben sent her a missive shortly after you left."

Amelia hadn't mentioned receiving a missive from Reuben, but then, she didn't tell him every single thing that happened to her. He would have to confirm this with Amelia before accusing Carol of lying.

"Did you talk to anyone while you were out?" So as not to arouse her suspicions, he added, "A walk all by yourself seems like it could be boring."

"I don't get bored when walking by myself. In fact, it gives me time to think without any distractions."

He resisted the urge to frown. She hadn't answered his question. She implied she didn't talk to anyone, but that didn't mean she hadn't run into someone while out. Perhaps she had run into Mr. Weber.

"Nothing of interest happened this afternoon," she continued as if she was in a hurry to end the conversation. "My afternoon was much more fun after I came home." She settled her head back on his shoulder and snuggled into his arms.

He thought about pressing the issue but decided against it. If she wasn't going to be forthcoming with her activities, he was going to have to find another way to discover if she was being unfaithful to him.

Chapter Sixteen

"I wish we were allowed more than two dances with the same partner at these balls," Amelia said the next morning as she cut into her waffle. "Why should I have to dance with anyone except Reuben?" She shot her brother a pointed look. "You can't tell me you didn't notice the way he doted over me at the ball."

"Yes, I noticed," Grant allowed, "but until you start reading banns with him, nothing is certain. For all we know, he might find someone he likes more."

"But who could he find that would be better than me?" Amelia turned her gaze to Carol. "Carol, tell Grant what you think."

Carol, who had been cutting Lucinda's waffle, looked over at Amelia. "What do you want?"

"Tell my brother that Reuben wants to marry me," Amelia insisted. "You can tell he's in love with me."

Carol's cheeks went pink. "Well, yes, but he hasn't come out and said anything. It's just something I detect about him."

Amelia gave Grant a satisfied smile. "I told you."

"Hate fork." Lucinda picked up the section of the waffle Carol hadn't cut up yet and shoved it into her mouth.

Amelia tried to hide her chuckle, but she was unsuccessful at the task. She quickly cleared her throat and focused on the meal in front of her.

"Lucinda, that is not how a lady eats," Grant told his daughter. "If you want to find a suitable husband, you can't pick up food and shove it into your mouth. You need to eat with utensils."

"Why?" Lucinda asked with her mouth full.

"You can't speak while food is in your mouth, either." Grant hid his frustration. He was trying to teach the girl good manners, but she seemed determined not to follow his advice.

"Why?" Lucinda asked again.

"For one," Carol began as she cleaned the crumbs that fell to her frock, "you will ruin your nice clothes." The maid came over to offer help, but Carol said, "I'd like to do this myself, if that's all right." She glanced over at Grant. "I want to learn how to be a good mother."

Grant nodded to let the maid know that Carol would take care of Lucinda. It was touching to see the way Carol acted around the girl. Amelia was good about helping him with the child, but no one could take a mother's place.

"Not hungry," Lucinda said as Carol finished wiping the food off of her clothes and face.

"Do you mind if I help her into another outfit?" Carol asked Grant.

"I think it'd be nice if you did," Grant replied with a smile.

She returned his smile. "Thank you. We'll be back soon."

Grant watched as Carol led her out of the room.

"It's sweet that she is trying so hard to be a good mother," Amelia commented. "But it's also good that Lucinda eats dinner before we do. Otherwise, poor Carol wouldn't get to eat an entire meal with us."

Grant had been hoping Carol would have to leave the room early so he could have a moment alone with his sister. He shifted in his chair and took a sip of water. "Carol said that Reuben sent you a missive yesterday."

Amelia's eyes lit up. "He did! Thank you for reminding me. I'm going to show it to you when we're done eating. Then you'll know he doesn't want to waste his time on any other lady. He wants to be with me."

He was too relieved to care that his sister, once again, had managed to bring the topic to Reuben. Carol had told him the truth. Reuben had sent a missive to Amelia yesterday. If she was telling him the truth about that, then she might have really gone for a walk by herself.

"Reuben gave me roses," she rambled with a blush on her cheeks. "They were naturally white, but he had them dyed so they were green and blue. He did that because of the blue and green cameo I was wearing that evening at the Duke of Creighton's ball. He said that since Lord Quinton had been so scared of it, he ended up being my dinner companion instead. That was a beautiful gesture. It means he loves me."

Grant blinked in horror. "Who was there to chaperone this visit? Don't tell me you were in the townhouse alone with him."

She shook her head in astonishment. "I can't believe you don't pay better attention when I tell you things. I just got through saying his sister-in-law was there to chaperone. We were not alone."

Grant relaxed. "I apologize. I missed that part."

"I suppose I can't be too rough with you. I'm sure you can't help but think of Carol. She's turning out to be a good wife for you. I'm not just saying that because she wants to be Lucinda's mother. I can tell she loves you in the same way I love Reuben."

His ears perked up in hope. "Can you?"

She nodded. "I wasn't sure if a sudden marriage could result in a love match. You two haven't known each other for long. I thought love would take time to develop. Maybe it depends on the people who are matched together." Amelia poked the fork into her waffle. "Carol can't stop staring at you when she thinks you aren't looking. I noticed the way she kept sneaking glances in your direction last night at the ball. I'm sure she was glad when you interrupted the conversation that gentleman was having with her and her friend."

So Amelia had seen Mr. Weber talking to Carol. "You think she was glad when I went over to her?"

"She looked relieved. That's how I feel whenever Lord Compton and Mr. Everson need to leave." She gave him a pointed look.

He should have known she would take the opportunity to let him know how much she didn't want to keep things going with her other suitors. "Do you know what your problem is, Amelia?" Before she could respond, he said, "Your problem is that once you have an idea in your head, you stick with it. For all we know, Reuben might be courting another lady. Until marriage is brought up, nothing is certain."

She groaned and popped the waffle into her mouth.

Carol returned with Lucinda. "Lucinda says she's not hungry anymore, and I think I've had enough to eat. Do you two mind if we wait for you in the drawing room?"

Grant looked down at his plate and decided he'd had enough to eat. Besides, he was getting tired of arguing with his sister about her suitors. He folded his napkin and set it on the plate. "I'm done. Perhaps we can go out for a walk."

"Animals!" Lucinda called out in excitement.

"No, we're not going back to the menagerie," Grant said before he had time to reflect on his answer.

The others around him blinked in surprise, though he was sure his sister was the most surprised in the group. She, after all, knew he had a tendency to carefully think before answering.

"I would rather take a stroll through the park," he hurried to say. "Maybe we could stop by some shops along the way."

Amelia's eyes lit up in excitement. "If you're going to do some shopping, I want to come! There was this adorable bonnet

I saw the other day. I promised myself if I still wanted it after a couple of days, I could get it. Do you mind if I get it?"

"I don't mind getting the bonnet for you," he said.

She clapped her hands together and jumped up from her chair. Noting the cloth napkin that had fallen from her lap, she hurried to retrieve it and placed it on the plate. "I just need to put on a different pair of slippers, and I'll meet you in the drawing room."

She hurried out of the room, and Lucinda started to go after her so Carol picked her up. "She'll be right back down," Carol told the girl. "You don't have to run after her."

Grant smiled. "Amelia has three gentlemen running after her. You'll have to wait in line, Lucinda, if you want to get her attention."

Carol laughed at his joke, and it warmed something deep within him to know she appreciated his humor. Now that he had spoken with Amelia, he felt much better. He even felt foolish for suspecting Carol might be interested in Mr. Weber.

She'd only been talking with her friend at the ball. Mr. Weber had been the one to approach her, not the other way around. He was certain if it hadn't been for his experience with Fiona, he never would have doubted Carol to begin with. He would have known Carol hadn't invited him to make advances toward her. It was good he hadn't pressed the issue with Carol last night. He would have ruined things between them, and they wouldn't have this pleasant day to look forward to. All he really had to do was watch Mr. Weber. As long as Mr. Weber stayed away from her, there wouldn't be any problems.

Chapter Seventeen

Amelia sighed in disappointment as she waved her fan to cool herself off. Carol glanced at the other six people in the drawing room to see if any of them had noticed Amelia's reaction to finding out Reuben wasn't able to attend the dinner party that evening, but it didn't seem like they had.

Carol caught the flicker of worry on Amelia's face and bit her lower lip. Should she ask why Reuben had chosen not to attend the dinner party, or would that be inappropriate?

"I don't mind being your escort for the evening," Horatio told Amelia. "Mr. St. George wasn't feeling well, so I told Warren and Malcolm that I would be your escort."

Carol couldn't be sure, but she thought she caught a flicker of interest for Amelia in Horatio's eyes. She'd known Horatio for years and couldn't recall a time he ever took an interest in anyone. There were times she and Rachel thought he might end up becoming a monk.

Amelia, who was sitting in the chair next to Carol, shifted in a way that let Carol know she wasn't all that comfortable with the match.

"I think the arrangement will work out well," Grant told his sister.

Amelia glanced at her brother in alarm. If Carol had to guess, the last thing Amelia wanted was another suitor, but Grant, being the dutiful brother, wanted to give her as many choices as possible. Carol realized Amelia wouldn't want to hear it, but she would have loved it if she'd had her choice of suitors. Given how well things were going with Grant, she would have picked him. But, just imagine the thrill of having gentlemen vying for a lady's hand in marriage. Amelia had no idea how lucky she was.

"We promise not to bore you ladies with details about the rail line," Mr. Malcolm Jasper spoke up with a wry grin. "We'll stick with topics that my wife enjoys. Regan, my dear, have you heard any good gossip lately?"

Malcolm's wife pretended to look appalled but the slight smile on her face betrayed her. "I think it's awful you would ask that in a room full of people I never met before. You should have waited until at least our second meeting to let them know how terrible I am." She winked at Carol and Amelia.

At once, Carol decided she liked Regan. The lady had marvelous wit. Deciding to play along, Carol said, "Have you heard about my friend, Miss Lydia Hamilton?"

Regan's eyes grew wide in interest. "The name seems familiar. Was she mentioned in the *Tittletattle*?"

"I'm not sure," Carol replied. "I don't read that paper."

Warren Beaufort, the Earl of Steinbeck, grimaced. "It's for the best you don't," he told Carol. "Not everything in it is true."

"How can you be sure of that?" Regan asked him.

"I'm not at liberty to say, but I recently found out many stories printed in that publication were all made up," he pointed out.

Regan's eyebrows furrowed. "You know this for a fact?"

Warren nodded. "Malcolm can confirm this."

Though Malcolm seemed reluctant to respond, he said, "It's true. You can't believe everything you read in the *Tittletattle*. Some of those stories are fables."

"The thing that happened with my friend is true," Carol told Regan when she caught the flicker of disappointment on the lady's face. "My friend ran off to elope with Lord Quinton. She's still gone. That makes it about three weeks since they left."

"Interesting," Regan said. "Considering the fact that they're not back yet, I'd say the elopement is going very well. Most of the time, couples return as soon as they're done with Gretna Green."

"That's because most marriages are done out of necessity rather than love," Iris, Lord Steinbeck's wife, replied.

"I don't know if Regan and I married for necessity," Malcolm began. "I think it was for practical reasons."

Regan smirked. "Yes, you were so eager to marry anyone but me that you sought the help of some matchmakers to find your bride."

Carol glanced between the two of them. "But the two of you are married."

"It just so happened that one of the matchmakers was his sister, and she thought I'd be good for him," Regan said. "He didn't know he married me until after the vows were exchanged."

Before Carol could ask her how she managed to work that part out, Malcolm interrupted, "It all worked out for the best. I'm very happy with the match."

"Things weren't all that wonderful when Iris and I first married, either," Warren added, "but, thankfully, she forgave me for the way I behaved."

"I'm glad you two married," Regan said. "She makes your dinner parties worth coming to."

Regan's teasing grin made the others laugh. Regan, it seemed, was the fun one in the group. She knew how to joke and make people feel comfortable. Carol envied that about her. Unless she was with her close friends, she didn't know what to say. Though she'd known Horatio for a long time, the two were never friends. He was just someone related to her dearest friend, Rachel. She was just now feeling like she could be herself around Grant and Amelia, but she couldn't blurt out what she was really thinking in a group this big.

She could never come out and ask why Regan joked about Iris making the dinner parties fun. Iris struck her as someone like herself, an unassuming wallflower. What could make such a lady bloom? She studied the way Warren bowed his head toward Iris and whispered to her. Iris' face flushed with pleasure, and she smiled. Carol averted her gaze in case they noticed her staring at them.

The butler came in to announce that dinner was served, so the couples went to the dining room. Carol spent most of the meal in silence. The gentlemen kept trying not to discuss the rail line, but one of them would say something that started up a discussion about the investment they were obviously excited about. Regan and Amelia would bring up something Carol found more interesting to get the conversation back on its proper course. Sometimes Regan would even tease the gentlemen for loving their investments more than the ladies at the table, to which the others laughed. Carol couldn't be sure, but she thought Iris enjoyed the discussion about the rail lines since she seemed to pay closer attention to the conversation when it went in that direction. After some time, Carol realized Iris never tried to steer the gentlemen off the topic like Regan and Amelia did.

Carol would have chimed in if she could think of anything interesting to say, but nothing came to mind. She didn't know why she had envisioned this evening going better when Grant asked her if she wanted to attend the dinner party. Would he be sorry he married her? Even Amelia, who had only met the others tonight, managed to come up with a few witty things to keep their interest. After this, Grant might not want to take her to another dinner party. And if he didn't want to do that, then how could they ever have a love match? She'd been so preoccupied with flirting with him that she hadn't thought to ask the Duchess of Ashbourne how to impress his friends so she could fit in with his crowd.

Carol did her best to play along with charades when it was time to play a game, but she'd never been very good at it. She couldn't seem to catch onto what the person was acting out as fast as the others around her. The longer the evening got, the greater her worry grew. By the time she could finally leave, her stomach was all up in knots. She settled into the carriage and wished she hadn't eaten so much during the meal. She was in serious danger of throwing it back up.

"I can't believe I wasted an entire evening," Amelia muttered after the carriage moved forward.

"How can you say that?" Grant asked. "I suspected Horatio took an interest in you when we went to his dinner party last month. Tonight, I know for a fact he did."

Amelia grimaced. "Don't say that, Grant. You know I'm not interested in him."

"Why not? He has money. He's good looking. He's intelligent. He has a title. He's nice."

"Yes, he is all of those things," she interrupted before he could say more. "But he's not Reuben. I wanted to spend tonight with Reuben. I'm terribly disappointed."

"Reuben can't help that he was ill," Carol spoke up.

"No one is blaming him for that," Amelia assured her. "I'll have to send him a missive to let him know I hope he feels better soon. I was just hoping to see him tonight."

Grant held his tongue for a few moments then said, "I don't mean to push you into something you don't want, but would you at least give Horatio a chance? You can't say he's boring like Mr. Everson and Lord Compton are."

Amelia blew a strand of hair out of her eyes and pulled the shawl closer around herself. "He's not boring. I found his stories entertaining. But he's not Reuben."

"I don't understand how you can prefer Reuben without giving Horatio a fair chance."

"There are some things you just feel for people when you meet them, Grant. I can't make myself be romantically interested in Horatio."

"You don't have a romantic interest in him because you've convinced yourself you can't have a romantic interest in him."

"Why must you be so logical about everything? Sometimes I wonder if you have any feelings."

"Of course, I have feelings. Everyone has feelings."

"If you have them, you don't show them."

Amelia wouldn't say that if she'd been alone with Grant in bed. He was a very warm and tender lover. But Carol didn't dare say that to Grant's sister.

Grant paused for a long moment then said, "I'm only looking out for your best interest. I'm your brother. It's my job."

"I understand you're doing what you believe is best for me, but at some point, you have to appreciate the fact that I'm grown up. I can decide which gentleman is best for me."

Though Grant didn't seem happy with her answer, he grew quiet.

If either Rachel or Lydia were in the carriage, they would lighten the mood. Rachel would impart something nice to say about both of them and probably finish it by pointing out how sibling relationships were special. Lydia wasn't as sentimental as Rachel, so she'd probably come up with something funny that would make everyone laugh. Carol, on the other hand, was at a loss for words. She didn't know what to say to help ease the situation.

The carriage finally came to a stop. Amelia left the carriage first and hurried to the townhouse. Carol caught the heavy sigh Grant emitted before he stepped out of the carriage. Carol glanced at the footman who was holding the door as Grant helped her down from the carriage. The footman hadn't heard Grant sigh. Only she had. Carol was rather impressed that Grant could mask his frustration so well. She supposed that was why Amelia had accused him of not having feelings.

Carol quietly walked with Grant up the steps to the townhouse. She wanted to ask him if he was disappointed in her since she'd barely managed to say more than a few sentences the whole evening, but she was afraid he'd say yes. If she was honest with herself, she'd rather not know. After dealing with her guardian and the Duke of Augustine, she actually preferred the bliss of ignorance.

Once they were in the townhouse, Grant relieved the servants from duty for the rest of the night and escorted Carol up the stairs. He had made it a habit of going to her bedchamber every night, but he'd always been in a better mood during those times.

Grant's steps slowed to a stop before he approached her bedchamber. Her stomach tensed, and she worried she might start feeling nauseous again.

Grant glanced down the hall in the direction where Amelia slept then whispered, "Would you be interested in sharing a bed tonight?"

At once, relief flooded over her. He hadn't given up on her despite her horrible performance at the dinner party. He was still willing to give their marriage a try.

Mindful to keep things private, she nodded. She didn't think Amelia could hear him since he had whispered, so she saw no reason to take her chances in saying something.

Grant led her to her bedchamber and followed her into the room. He shut the door then turned to her. "I apologize for the way things ended this evening."

She blinked in surprise. He was apologizing to her?

"I didn't mean to get into an argument with Amelia right there in the carriage," he explained as he removed his frock coat and hat. "Sometimes she's so determined to get her way that it leaves no room for compromise. I really don't want it to ruin our night." He placed the items on a vacant part of her dresser.

She debated whether or not to confess what her worries over the evening had been, but in the next instant, he had her in his arms and was kissing her. Deciding to let the matter go, she kissed him in return. It didn't matter what her fear had been because her fear had not been realized. She hadn't ruined things between them by not being more social this evening. He still wanted to be with her.

Tomorrow, she would send the Duchess of Ashbourne a missive. Perhaps the duchess could help her figure out how to be more engaging at dinner parties. She'd been given a reprieve tonight, but she didn't want to repeat her lackluster performance at the next dinner party they were invited to. Next time, she'd like to do a better job of fitting in.

It was ironic if one thought about it. The entire time she'd been betrothed to the Duke of Augustine, she hadn't cared if she'd disappointed him or not. She hadn't been in danger of losing his affection because he'd never cared for her to begin with. But she had the very real possibility of a love match with Grant, and she wanted to do everything within her power to obtain it. One little slip could make all the difference. Yes, she would send the duchess a missive first thing tomorrow.

Grant lifted her up and carried her to the bed, and, for the moment, all of her worries were forgotten.

Chapter Eighteen

The next day, Carol sent off a missive as soon as she had a moment to herself. As it turned out, Grant hadn't gone off to visit one of his friends. Instead, he had asked Carol if she would like to join him and Lucinda for a stroll through the park. She wasn't about to decline such an invitation. After the stroll, Grant took her and Lucinda to the market and bought them both gifts. For Lucinda, he bought a doll with a gown that matched the color of her frock. For Carol, he bought flowers and a cameo.

When they returned, Grant received word from Lord Steinbeck about the railway investment. Grant promised to come back as soon as he was finished before he gave her a kiss so long that it made her weak in the knees. While Lucinda played with her doll, Carol wrote the missive and had the footman send it off. Then she shared crumpets and tea with Lucinda as she waited for Grant to return.

"That's a nice doll your father bought you today," Carol told Lucinda.

Lucinda showed her the color of the doll's dress. "Like red."

"Yes, red is a nice color." And the doll was good quality. This wasn't cheap like some of the toys she'd seen. But then, her cameo had cost quite a bit, too. "Your father is going to spoil us if he's not careful."

"What's 'spool'?"

Carol's lips turned up at the cute way Lucinda had mispronounced the word 'spoil'. "'Spoil' means to pamper." When Lucinda's eyebrows furrowed in confusion, she realized her definition hadn't clarified things. "Um, let me think…" She couldn't use the word 'indulge' because the girl probably didn't know what that word meant, either. "I'm not sure how to explain it, exactly, but it's like getting so many toys that you don't know what to do with them all. Your father is giving us a lot of things."

"Like doll."

"And I like the cameo and flowers he got me. I'm not saying that he's giving us bad things. Everything he's given us is wonderful. I think it's very sweet of him."

It was probably his way of showing them that he cared about them. Carol's gaze went to the flowers on the table in front of her. Then she touched the cameo she had pinned to her gown. She cherished both gifts immensely, especially since it was an expression of Grant's feelings for her.

The butler stepped into the room, and she lowered her hand from the cameo as she straightened up in the settee.

"You have a visitor, my lady," he said.

Her first thought was that Helena had come by, but that didn't make any sense. For one, Helena would have sent a missive. She was running a business. She wouldn't show up without making an appointment. And two, Carol doubted Helena would come by here since Carol didn't want Grant to know she was paying the lady to teach her how to make him fall in love with her. It'd be terribly embarrassing if he were to find that out. Certainly, Helena would be discreet.

Maybe it was Reginald. News of Grant's newfound relationship with Lord Steinbeck and Mr. Jasper was quickly spreading through London. Just that morning at Hyde Park, someone had stopped Grant to congratulate him on being able to secure a meeting with the two gentlemen. Reginald might come here in hopes that Grant would bring him to one of the meetings in the future. It would mean good money for him.

Carol forced aside the panic that threatened to rise up within her as she asked, "Who is it?"

"There are two ladies," the butler began. "Lady Rachel and Lady Quinton."

Carol relaxed. "Bring them in." As she rose to her feet, she quickly added, "We'll need two more cups, please."

The butler left, and Lucinda looked up at her. "Like them?" Lucinda asked.

"They're my friends. I like them very much."

"Like Papa?"

Face warm, she nodded. "Yes, I like him, too."

A movement caught Carol's attention, so she turned her attention back to the doorway. As the butler had said, Rachel and Lydia were here for a visit.

"The rumors are true," Rachel said as she and Lydia settled into their chairs. "Lydia is married."

Lydia chuckled. "And happily so. But, as Rachel pointed out on our way here, I'm not the only one who is happy. It seems you've taken on a certain glow since your marriage to Lord Wright."

Carol's face grew warmer. "Grant is much better than the Duke of Augustine."

Rachel gave a knowing look in Lydia's direction. "I told you she's in love with him."

Lydia smiled. "That is a relief. I know how much you were dreading a marriage to the duke. How did this marriage with Grant come about?"

"Rachel's brother suggested he marry me," Carol said.

Lydia glanced at Rachel. "Are you telling me that Horatio didn't want to marry Carol, either?"

"We've known each other for so long that Horatio thinks of you both as sisters," Rachel replied.

The butler came into the room and set out two cups and a fresh pot of tea. They waited for him to leave before resuming their conversation.

"I never fancied Horatio," Lydia said. "I wouldn't have married him even if he was interested in me."

Carol poured tea into their cups. "I didn't care for him that way, either. However, I would have married him if it meant I could get out of marriage to the Duke of Augustine." She handed them the cups then offered Lucinda another crumpet. "I'm very happy with the gentleman I ended up marrying."

"I should say so," Lydia commented after she sipped her tea. "You've never smiled so much in your life." She gave Rachel a wink. "You're also glowing."

Now it was Rachel's turn to blush. "Edwin is every bit the gentleman. I knew my secret admirer would be perfect for me."

"Yes, you did tell us that." Carol took a look at Lucinda. This conversation couldn't be all that interesting to a child, but she was happily eating the crumpet and admiring her doll. "Rachel, Lydia, this is Lucinda. I'm her new mother." She smiled at the girl. "Lucinda, these are my dear friends. We've known each other since we were children."

Rachel nodded. "We weren't as young as you when we met. I believe we were seven. Maybe eight?"

"I was eight, but you two were seven," Lydia said. "But we're only months apart in age."

"We met at Hyde Park," Carol added. "I caught Lydia pulling some flowers from a bush. I didn't want Lydia to get into trouble, so I went to warn her to stop. Rachel happened to be on the other side of the bush and gave me quite the scare when I noticed her."

Rachel laughed. "I wasn't trying to scare you."

Carol grinned. "I know. Anyway, my father and their mothers thought the three of us got along well and arranged for us to get together on a regular basis."

"Who knew flower theft could lead to a friendship?" Lydia joked.

The three friends chuckled.

"I don't think they really mind if you take a couple of flowers at the park," Rachel said. "Though I do agree Lydia shouldn't have taken so many."

Lydia shrugged. "I was a child. I thought it would be fun to decorate my bedchamber with a lot of flowers. With two brothers stinking up the place, the flowers would have made the place smell better."

"Oh, that's not fair," Rachel admonished. "Felix was always careful about how he smelled. Even to this day, he likes everything clean. Does he still take two baths a day?"

"No. And it's not from lack of wanting them. It's just that when you have to heat up the water and put it into a tub yourself, you realize you can go without two baths a day. I doubt he'll go back to that habit even after we hire a house full of servants."

Carol's eyes widened. "So Lord Quinton is willing to help your family out financially?"

"Yes," Lydia began. "I knew Guy was a sweet and loving person when I met him. Every moment I've spent with him has been wonderful. He's attentive to my every need, and even though he doesn't always get along with my brothers, he looks out for them for my sake. He even protects me when he thinks my sensibilities will be offended. He is the perfect husband."

Rachel shook her head, not hiding her surprise. "I wouldn't have guessed that by the way he behaved at the dinner party."

The more Carol heard about this dinner party the two had attended, the more she wished she'd been there. It sounded like a memorable evening.

"I wished we could have stayed in the country longer, but we were forced to return early," Lydia continued. She paused then glanced in Lucinda's direction. "I have something to tell you both that isn't appropriate to say in front of a child. I hate to ask this of you, Carol, but do you mind sending the maid to watch her?"

Carol hesitated but then figured the poor girl had to be bored. They weren't saying anything that could possibly interest a child. With a nod, she got up from the settee and went to the cord to summon the maid.

When she returned to the group, Lucinda said, "Want to stay."

Carol blinked in surprise. Lucinda wasn't bored? Carol glanced at Lydia, silently asking her friend if the news she had to share was so sensitive that they needed to send Lucinda to another room. Lydia gave Carol a look that told her the news really was that serious.

Carol turned her attention back to Lucinda, who was looking up at her with hope that she could stay in the room. This wasn't easy. She was still new to being a mother. How would a parent handle this situation? Her father had doted on her, but it'd been so long ago that she didn't remember if she'd ever asked to stay when he had to discuss something serious with an adult. Reginald would have just told her she needed to be quiet and do what she was told, and he would have done that in a gruff way. It was a shame Grant wasn't here. Based on how he handled things with his sister, he would know the right balance between being kind but firm.

After a long moment, Carol placed a comforting hand on the girl's back. "I'm sorry, but I'm afraid this is something you're not old enough to know."

Lucinda frowned. "Not happy."

Carol winced. Up to now, she had been able to do whatever the girl wanted. She didn't realize it would hurt to tell her no.

The maid came into the room.

Carol almost told the maid to forget it, but another look at Lydia let her know how much her friend wanted to share this news with her. With a sigh, Carol apologized, again, to the girl before asking the maid to take her upstairs.

Lucinda pouted but went with the maid.

Carol felt awful. She'd be lucky if the girl wanted to sit next to her ever again.

"All right, Lucinda is out of the room, and you refused to tell me anything until we came here," Rachel told Lydia. "What is it that you want to tell us?"

"Did you hear about the Duke of Ivandore?" Lydia asked.

Carol's eyebrows furrowed. She hadn't heard anything about the Duke of Ivandore. She didn't even know who the Duke of Ivandore was. Her gaze went to Rachel to see if her friend knew this gentleman Lydia referred to.

Rachel gasped. "He's not Lady Elizabeth's brother, is he?"

"Who's Lady Elizabeth?" Carol blurted out.

"Don't you read the *Tittletattle*?" Rachel asked.

"You know I don't concern myself with the gossip papers. It's nothing but idle talk."

"Well, if you read it, you'd know who Lady Elizabeth is. The whole Ton is appalled by the rumors going around about her. I don't know whether to feel sorry for her or not. If the rumors are true, then she deserves to be shunned, but if they're not, then the people spreading the rumors need to be ashamed of themselves."

Lydia cleared her throat. "Funny you should say that because Felix is the one who started those rumors."

Rachel put her hand over her mouth then said, "He didn't! Why, he ought to be ashamed of himself. And you should be ashamed of him, as well. How could you marry Guy in order to save his estate? He deserves to live in poverty for the rest of his life. He ruined Lady Elizabeth. Her brother had to take her out of London because the rumors are so bad."

"I'm not going to apologize for what Felix did," Lydia interrupted before Rachel could continue. "I know what he did was wrong. But he was drunk at the time, and he swears all he said was that she's had quite a few gentlemen in her bed, has a bit of a temper, and that she's not very smart."

Rachel rolled her eyes. "Oh, is that all he said?"

"That is all very terrible," Carol agreed. "You can't defend that, Lydia. I don't care if he was drunk or not."

"I'm not defending him," Lydia replied. "My point is that he didn't say the other things that people are saying about her. In my opinion, those things are far worse."

"What else could they possibly be saying?" Carol asked.

Rachel lowered her voice and said, "They're suggesting she will debase herself with animals. The latest article in the *Tittletattle* suggested that she has sold her soul to the Devil. An unknown source told the *Tittletattle* that a book full of dark magic rituals was delivered to her townhouse the other day. She's even been said to have drawn a pig being sacrificed on an altar."

Carol couldn't believe her ears. "They are saying all of that about a single person?"

Lydia gestured to Carol. "That proves my point, Rachel. Who can be guilty of all of these things? No one. It's ridiculous that so many people believe all of this nonsense. When I left London, all they were saying was that she had loose morals."

"That doesn't exonerate Felix for what he did," Rachel said.

"I'm not trying to exonerate him," Lydia argued. "I'm only saying that he isn't as bad as you think. Yes, he has his part to blame, but he isn't responsible for all of this. The people spreading rumors have made things worse."

"Well, is he going to do the right thing and tell everyone he started this?"

"Yes. That's why we came back to London early. He's here to make things right. He's going to marry her once he gets the matter about her brother's death settled."

Carol's eyes widened. "Her brother died?" Could life get any worse for this poor lady? She'd thought her life had been pretty awful while living under her guardian's thumb, but that was nothing compared to this.

Lydia nodded. "Felix, Oscar, and I took Guy to my family's estate in order to stop her brother from forcing Felix into a duel. We had planned to return to London after the Duke of Ivandore left for America with Lady Elizabeth. Unfortunately, the Duke of Ivandore followed us and tried to kill Felix out there." Lydia paused and glanced at her friends. "Isn't that terrible?"

"To be honest, I'm sympathetic toward the Duke of Ivandore," Rachel replied after a long silence fell upon the group.

Lydia huffed. "Felix is my brother."

"I know, but look at the damage he caused," Rachel said.

Sensing the two were about to get into an argument, Carol inserted, "Did the Duke of Ivandore and Felix have a duel then?"

Lydia nodded. "I don't know the details, but the two got into a sword fight, and Felix killed him." She shot Rachel a pointed look. "It was in defense. The duke was chasing him through the manor. I saw it for myself. Felix ran up the stairs. The duke followed after him. At the time, Felix had nothing in his hands, and the duke had a sword. What was Felix supposed to do? Just stand there and let the duke pierce him with the sword?"

"Of course, I don't think Felix should just let the duke kill him," Rachel began. "Felix had a right to defend himself. But I can understand why the duke was so angry. What Felix did was inexcusable. What compelled him to say all of this about the poor lady?"

Yes, Carol wanted to know that, too. She'd never spent much time around him, but she didn't think he was the type of person to go around ruining people's reputations.

"Guy told me that Felix asked her to dance at a ball, and she said no," Lydia said.

Carol's eyebrows furrowed. "Are we allowed to say no if a gentleman asks us to dance?"

"My brother always said that I should be polite and say yes," Rachel replied. "Though he did say that if I let him fill out my dance card, then he could find a reason to decline a dance. He said he could tell the gentleman that my dance card was full. That way, we could avoid hurting anyone's feelings."

"Did this lady have a dance card?" Carol asked.

Lydia shrugged. "I have no idea. All I know is that Felix went to her directly, she said no, and he ended up going to some gentleman's club where he got drunk. That's where he started the rumors, and now those rumors have been added to by other people. Felix realizes the error of his ways. Once the judge clears him of murder, he intends to propose to Lady Elizabeth."

"I'll be surprised if she says yes," Rachel said.

"She might not have any choice but to agree to it," Carol inserted. "Who else is going to marry her?"

Rachel thought for a moment then grimaced. "Probably no one. Oh, I feel so sorry for her."

"I do, too," Lydia assured her. "I don't envy her position. She's trapped. I wish her brother had taken her to America where she could have gotten a new start. It would have been better for her. She's going to have to live with this forever."

"Hopefully, it won't be that long," Carol said. "I can't believe that people will go on believing all of those things. At some point, they'll have to realize everything has been exaggerated."

Rachel sipped her tea then asked, "Is Felix going to tell everyone that he started the rumors?"

Lydia nodded. "As we speak, he's at the same gentleman's club where he started the rumors. He's telling them that he made up those lies. He'll be going to a lawyer with Guy and Oscar after he's done. They already took the duke's body to the proper authority yesterday. I would have seen you two sooner except we got in late last night."

Carol sat back in the settee. Even now, she was having trouble comprehending it all. "I thought Rachel had the most exciting story to tell, what with her falling in love and eloping with a servant, but you tell a tale that can fill up an entire book."

"Your news is exciting, too," Rachel argued. "You didn't have to marry the Duke of Augustine, and, better yet, you're happy with Grant."

"Yes, but it's not as dramatic as what Lydia's going through," Carol said.

"I'm not going through it," Lydia interrupted. "My brother is. Everything between me and Guy has gone smoothly. It turns out he fancied me at Horatio's dinner party. He was going to ask to be my suitor once it became spring."

"Why wait for spring?" Rachel asked in surprise.

"Because spring is a lucky time of year compared to winter," Lydia answered as if her statement was based on fact.

"I can't wait for you to meet her husband," Rachel told Carol. "You won't believe how strange he is until you meet him for yourself."

"That's not fair," Lydia protested. "We all have our own way of doing things that seem strange to others."

Rachel chuckled. "Yes, but most of us aren't scared of being paired up with someone who wears a certain color."

Lydia rolled her eyes.

"At least they love each other," Carol told Rachel. "That's what matters, doesn't it?"

"I suppose so," Rachel replied, and though she tried to appear serious, Carol caught a hint of laughter in her voice.

"I grow tired of all of this," Lydia said. "Why don't we go shopping? My husband thinks I should go to the market and pamper myself."

"Can we bring Lucinda?" Carol asked, thinking that it might help make the girl feel better if she was included in the outing. Yes, she and Grant had taken her to the market earlier that day, but she was sure Lucinda would rather go back there than be left here.

Lydia and Rachel agreed to bring her, and Rachel added, "Won't it be fun when we all have children to take with us to the market?"

Lydia's eyes lit up. "We can shop for their clothes together. Oh! Carol already has a daughter. We should get something nice for her to wear. We could get her a cute little bonnet or maybe a pretty frock with some lace on it."

Carol supposed it would be fine if they got Lucinda something. Earlier that day at the market, Grant said all she needed to do was tell the merchant he would pay for the things she purchased, and he'd added that she was welcome to buy something for their daughter. *Their daughter.* It was still taking her time to get used to being a mother. Taking Lucinda out with her friends might help with that. Excited, Carol hurried to get her.

Chapter Nineteen

Grant returned from his meeting with Lord Steinbeck to a quiet townhouse. "Where are Lady Wright and my daughter?" he asked the butler.

"They went to the market with Lady Rachel and Lady Quinton," the butler replied from the doorway of the drawing room. "They left a half hour ago. Lady Wright didn't say when they expected to be back."

If Carol was anything like Amelia, she would shop with her friends for hours. He supposed there was no point in sticking around the drawing room and waiting for her like some lovesick fool. He wouldn't have run off to see Lord Steinbeck if the matter hadn't been important. His first responsibility was to the wellbeing of the estate. His second was to himself.

He went to the library to update his ledger. When he was done with that, he picked a book from one of the shelves. A few pages into the thing, he realized he couldn't focus on it. What he most wanted to do was spend time with Carol. He glanced at the clock and saw that he'd only been in this room for forty-five minutes. That couldn't have been enough time for her to be done shopping with her friends. But she did take Lucinda with her, so maybe having a child there would shorten the trip.

He shut the book. He almost put it back on the shelf but decided to take it with him to the drawing room. Even if he couldn't focus on it, he might as well use it so no one realized he was really waiting for Carol to return.

He spent the next hour sipping tea and unsuccessfully trying to read the book. When he caught sight of someone finally entering the drawing room, he looked up from the book. It was Amelia. He hid his disappointment.

Amelia turned to her lady's maid and said, "Thank you for coming with me today."

Her lady's maid offered a nod then left.

His gaze met Amelia's, and at once, he knew she was going to tell him something he wouldn't like. Well, there was no sense in putting on a pretense of reading a book under these circumstances. He closed it and rose to his feet as she approached him. "What did you do?"

"I'm not going to marry Lord Compton or Mr. Everson," she began with a resolute tone in her voice. "Not only do I find them boring, but I'm not the least bit attracted to them. I see no reason to keep letting them court me. Their time and attention will be better spent on ladies who fancy them. I went to their residences and ended the courtships. I brought my lady's maid to act as chaperone, so you needn't worry about my reputation. I would have asked Carol to go with me, but I didn't want to put her in the uncomfortable position of doing something she knows you wouldn't like."

Grant bit his tongue so he wouldn't speak before he had a chance to think. Despite everything he'd told her, she refused to appreciate the fact that it was a luxury to have a line of suitors vying for her hand in marriage.

"Give me a moment," he requested before he made his way to one of the windows.

He needed to put some distance between them so he could think clearly. He was upset. And understandably so. This could very well ruin her chances of a good marriage. Reuben might never propose. He was unpredictable. Sometimes he showed up at social events, and sometimes he didn't. Though he had asked to be her suitor, he hadn't come by as much as the other two gentlemen. All of that showed a lack of dedication. How could she be so reckless as to put all of her hopes on him?

He tapped the book on the palm of his hand. Of all the foolish things she could have done, why did it have to be this? Once word of this got out, the honorable bachelors would stop trying to woo her. Then she'd be left with the questionable ones if things didn't go as she hoped with Reuben.

Grant turned back to face her. "Are you prepared to accept the consequences of what you did today? You might end up being a spinster. This is your second Season."

She nodded. "I thought long and hard about this, Grant, and this is the right decision."

"What if Reuben doesn't propose?"

"He will. I'm certain of it."

"How? He hasn't come to me to discuss marriage. He only asked to court you. Mr. Everson and Lord Compton, on the other hand, expressed an interest in marrying you. I asked them to give you more time before proposing."

Her face went white. "Then it's a good thing I ended those courtships. I would have told them both no."

"Why? What's so wrong about being with a gentleman who's boring or not as handsome as others? These were decent, stable gentlemen. Their finances are secure, and they will be faithful. They'll make you comfortable."

"If I marry comfortable, I'll spend the rest of my life pining away for someone else, and if I find someone who does interest me, I'll be tempted to take him as a lover."

He blinked, shocked she would come out and echo the same thing Fiona had told him when he confronted her about the affair she'd had with the cook. *I never loved you, Grant. The truth is, I found you tedious, but my father wanted us to marry, so I married you. Looking back, I realize I should have said yes to the gentleman I really wanted, even if my father didn't approve the match. If I had done that, then we would have been spared this misery.*

"I did them a kindness today," Amelia continued. "I'm sorry if you can't see that, but I was thinking of what is best for them when I ended those courtships."

Amelia started to head out of the room when Grant stopped her. She halted and turned back to face him.

Grant let out a heavy sigh and stopped tapping the book on the palm of his hand. "You're right. You did do them a kindness. You don't want a cold marriage. No husband wants to end up hearing that his wife has taken a lover because he doesn't interest her."

She relaxed. "Thank you for understanding."

A moment of silence passed between them before he asked, "If things don't work out with Reuben, will you consider Horatio? He's still interested in you."

She winced, and at once, he knew she wouldn't. As she had told him before, if she couldn't have Reuben, she didn't want anyone.

He gripped the book with both hands. "I can't help but feel sorry for all of the boring gentlemen out there."

"Well, you wouldn't know anything about being boring. Fiona was the boring one in your marriage to her."

If only she knew… But he would rather she didn't know. In fact, he would prefer that no one ever find out about him and Fiona.

"You and Carol are a perfect match," Amelia went on. "I can only hope I get to enjoy the kind of marriage you two do." She smiled. "I know it might not seem like it, but I do value your opinion. I didn't like the way things ended last night between us. I want us to get along."

After a moment, he returned her smile. "I want that, too."

"I'll let you get back to your book. I'm going to take a nap. I barely slept last night. I'll see you and Carol at dinner."

He offered her a nod before she left the room. His gaze went to his book. He didn't know if he felt like keeping up the pretense of reading. The book was a good one. He just wasn't in the mood to read. He wanted Carol to come home.

He leaned against the wall next to the window and watched the people who passed by. If it happened that Carol returned from her outing, he would slip out of view so she wouldn't catch him waiting for her. It was bad enough ladies had nothing but disdain for boring gentlemen. He didn't need Carol to know he would rather spend time looking out the window to see when she came home than reading a good book.

After a few minutes, a lad who looked to be about ten stopped in front of his townhouse and came up the steps.

Curious, Grant beat the footman to the front door. "I'll get it," he told him. He waited until the footman was gone before he opened the door. "May I help you?"

"Is this the residence of Lady Wright?" the lad asked.

"Yes. Who wants to know?"

The lad shrugged. "Some duchess. I can't pronounce the full title. I am to deliver this to Lady Wright. Is she here?"

"Lady Wright isn't available at the moment. I'll give it to her."

"My apologies, mister, but I'm not sure I can do that. The duchess insisted I give it only to Lady Wright."

Grant frowned. That was odd. Why should it matter if he took the correspondence? "I'm Lord Wright. I don't think the duchess will mind if I give it to my wife."

The lad's eyebrows furrowed. "I don't know if I can do that."

"Sure, you can. I'm her husband. Under the law, we are one."

"I don't care what the law says. I've been paid to deliver this, in person, to only Lady Wright. I'll get in trouble if I give this to anyone else."

"You won't get in trouble if I don't mention this to anyone."

The lad fidgeted. "While that's true, how do I know you won't tell someone?"

Grant didn't like the way this conversation was going. He didn't think that a boy this young would be trying to get more money by holding off on giving him the correspondence. He would assume this of an older boy. But even if this lad learned the art of manipulation early on, Grant wanted to see what someone was trying to keep from him. After what he went through with Fiona, he had a right to know if his wife was keeping a secret from him.

Grant dug into his pocket. "I think I have some money I can give you in exchange for that missive."

"But, my lord, I've already been paid. And handsomely so. I can't take your money."

Grant felt the knot in his stomach tighten. He most definitely had to see what was in that envelope. Perhaps it wasn't from a duchess. Perhaps it was from a Mr. Weber. He let go of the coins in his pocket. "All right, I'll bring Lady Wright here. You will come in and wait?"

The lad nodded and stepped into the entryway.

Grant scanned the street and sidewalk to make sure Carol wasn't nearby then shut the door. The irony wasn't lost on him. He'd spent the past hour and a half hoping Carol would show up, and now that this lad was here, he was praying she would be delayed.

"I'll be right back," he told the lad then hurried up the stairs to his sister's bedchamber. He knocked on the door. "Amelia, I need your help with something, and I need it now."

After a couple of agonizing seconds, she opened the door. Her hair had been unpinned and needed to be brushed, but she was still fully dressed. "What's wrong?"

"I need you to pretend to be Carol and take a missive from this lad that's downstairs. But you can't tell anyone about this."

Amelia laughed. "Is this a joke?"

"No, I'm very serious." He waved for her to leave her bedchamber. "The lad can't stay here." Not when Carol could arrive at any moment. "Come on."

Though she appeared confused, she stepped into the hall and followed him. "All right, but do you mind telling me why you're doing this?"

Grant didn't want to tell her, but he also didn't want her to tell Carol, and she might do that if he didn't give her a good reason to keep silent on the issue. "At the last ball, there was this gentleman who was interested in Carol. I'm afraid it's from him."

"Oh, there's no way Carol would have an affair. She's in love with you."

As much as he'd like to believe his sister, he couldn't be sure until he read the contents of that missive. "The lad refuses to give the missive to anyone but Carol. Don't you find that strange?"

"Did he say who sent the missive?"

"He claims it's from a duchess, but he conveniently can't pronounce the lady's title. Don't you find that suspicious?"

"Not all titles are easy to pronounce. But I agree this whole thing is strange."

Since they were close to the entryway, he whispered, "That's why I need you to keep this between us. I don't want anyone to find out."

"Not even Carol?" she whispered in return.

"Not even her." Ignoring the flicker of apprehension that crossed her face, he led her over to the lad. "Here you are," he told the lad. "This is Lady Wright."

Amelia's attention went to the lad. "My husband said you have a missive for me."

The lad handed it to her. "My apologies, my lord and lady, but I was bound by my word to give this to Lady Wright and no one else. I meant no disrespect."

Grant shot Amelia a pointed look. Surely, she could see why he required her secrecy now.

Amelia offered the lad a smile. "I appreciate the fact that you kept your word. It tells me you're going to grow up to be a man of character. Thank you for the missive."

Grant glanced back at Amelia to make sure she didn't open the envelope as he saw the lad out the door. If there was something going on, he'd rather she not know the details. If there was an affair going on, it would be difficult to keep her from finding out about it. Mr. Weber might think he was being clever by sending a missive as a "duchess" and only allowing Carol to receive it. If Grant hadn't gone through infidelity in his first marriage, he might have fallen for the ruse. Back then, he blindly believed whatever people told him. He knew better now, though. It was to his advantage that the lad had no idea who they were so Amelia could play the part of Lady Wright.

Grant closed the door then took the missive from his sister. "For your willingness to keep quiet about this, I will tell Horatio that you are considering a proposal from Reuben. That's not a complete lie. You are considering what you'll say if he does propose."

"Oh, I don't need to consider it. I'll tell him yes. But I understand what you're doing, and I appreciate it. Yes, please tell Horatio that so he doesn't put me in the difficult position of having to tell him no."

"I'll relay the message when I see him."

"Thank you." She kissed his cheek. "I hope whatever you find in that missive won't upset you."

He waited until she went back up the stairs before he returned to the drawing room. He gave a quick glance out the window to make sure Carol wasn't anywhere in sight before he opened the envelope.

In it was a message that, for the most part, was blank. It was from someone claiming to be Helena. The person had only written down a date and time. His gaze went to the address printed on the stationary. He frowned. This didn't look good. He'd been right to keep this from Amelia. She didn't need to know that someone—Mr. Weber, perhaps—was pretending to be a lady in order to get Carol to meet with him tomorrow at two in the afternoon.

What a clever ploy Mr. Weber had chosen. Carol probably knew someone by the name Helena. Mr. Weber might have probed into the circle of her friends and was using this to get her attention. A husband who didn't know better would never suspect his wife was being asked for a secret rendezvous by something this secretive.

Well, Mr. Weber, I do happen to know better. And tomorrow you'll find that out when I see you in person at two o'clock.

Chapter Twenty

Carol returned home an hour later with Lucinda and her friends. The poor girl was exhausted. She ended up falling asleep before the carriage came to a stop.

"I didn't realize we were out for so long," Lydia said.

"I don't know what excites you more," Rachel teased as she gestured to the boxes next to her on the seat. "You are in love with Guy, but I notice you bought so many things we have a couple of packages inside this carriage."

"Guy insisted I get an entire wardrobe," Lydia replied. "I just hope I picked the right colors. Our marriage got off to a wonderful start. I don't want to jeopardize that."

"So that's why you didn't get anything red, yellow-green, or black," Carol said. While shopping, she kept wondering why her friend had been selective about the colors of the gowns, hats, bonnets, slippers, and gloves. Her friend hadn't been that picky before. Now it made sense.

"I hope Guy agrees to host a dinner party so Carol can meet him," Rachel said. "I'd like to know what she thinks of him."

Lydia frowned. "You only want her to meet him so you two can have fun at his expense."

"That's not true." Though Rachel spoke those words, Carol suspected that Rachel's motives were for her to see how strange Guy was.

But Carol didn't care what the motives were. If she was able to attend a dinner party with her friends, she would have something to talk about. Then she wouldn't seem so boring to Grant. "I'd love to go to a dinner party." She turned her hopeful eyes to Lydia. "I don't care how strange Guy is. I just want to have a dinner with my friends. Grant's sister is nice, but being with her at a dinner party isn't the same as being with you two."

"Oh, all right," Lydia agreed as the footman opened the door. "But if I hear anyone say something unflattering about my husband, I'll fake an illness so everyone has to go home early."

"That's fair," Rachel conceded.

Carol made sure she had a firm hold on Lucinda before she carried her out of the carriage. She turned back to Lydia. "When will you be sending the invite?"

"I'll send an invitation when I know what day works for Guy." She glanced at Rachel as if she expected Rachel to make some comment, and when Rachel didn't say anything, she relaxed.

"I don't think Grant has anything planned with his friends for the next week," Carol said.

"I'll see what I can do. A week won't give Guy much time to decide which day will be best. There are many things he has to factor in."

"He has that many friends?"

"Well, no. It's not that his social calendar is full. It's just that he's," Lydia glanced at Rachel, "selective about the days he does things."

Rachel smirked.

Lydia groaned. "That's the thing you better not do at the dinner party. So what if he's particular about what day he does something on? He'll be a good host."

Rachel's cheeks grew pink. "I'm sorry. I suppose it still bothers me that he made everyone switch partners because of a green and blue cameo."

"Well, he can't switch partners now. I'm his wife, and you two are already married. We're coming to this dinner party already matched up."

Carol waited to see if her friends would say more, but they didn't. Seeing that as a good time to say goodbye, she did. The footman followed her up to her townhouse with a box of two new frocks and a bonnet for Lucinda. She had to admit it had been fun shopping for her, and she had even called her "Mama" during the afternoon's outing. She didn't realize how pleased she'd be to hear someone call her that. What excited her more was knowing she might someday have more children to call her that, too.

To her surprise, Grant greeted her at the door. He took Lucinda from her then told the footman to leave the box in the entryway. "Would you like some tea?"

"Yes, I would," she admitted. She hadn't had much to drink the entire afternoon.

"Go on to the drawing room, and I'll see to it that the tea you like will be prepared. I'll take Lucinda up to her room." He paused and glanced at the box. "Is that yours?"

"It's for Lucinda. We found two frocks and a bonnet she liked."

"I'll take that up with me, too, if you'll hand it to me. Why don't you go on to the drawing room? I'm looking forward to hearing all about your day."

Excited he wanted to spend time with her, she hurried to do as he wished. It really was quite wonderful to come back after spending time with her friends to a husband who seemed genuinely happy to see her. This was so different than what her life would have been if she'd had to marry the Duke of Augustine.

Once in the drawing room, she settled onto the settee. Her mind unwittingly went back to the afternoon she'd had those lessons with Helena. She hadn't been sure if they would work, but after she sat on this very settee and used a couple of the tricks Helena had taught her, he'd started kissing her. And he hadn't stopped there. He'd taken her up to his bedchamber and made love to her. Even now, her body tingled in the most pleasant way from the memory. She didn't suppose there would be time to see if she could get the same result if she employed those techniques again. Her gaze went to the clock. She sighed in disappointment. It was too late in the afternoon. They would have to get ready for dinner soon.

She turned her attention to the rest of the room. It wasn't decorated with many things, but it was still warm and receptive. She thought it fit Grant very well. She imagined if Amelia owned the place, there would be decorations all over the room. He might not be as forthcoming with his emotions as Amelia was, but there was nothing wrong with that. Not everyone wore their heart on their sleeve.

The butler came in with the tea and set it on the table in front of her.

Recalling the missive she had sent to Helena earlier that day, she asked, "Did a missive come for me while I was out?"

He shook his head. "No, my lady."

She should have known it would take Helena at least one full day before getting back to her. Helena was busy. She had a lot of clients. Carol wasn't the only one she was helping. Having gone to Helena, Carol realized how valuable the lady's guidance was. She was worth waiting for.

Carol waited until the butler left before she poured tea into two cups. She didn't think there were any impending dinner parties coming up where she had to worry about making a good impression. Hopefully, by the time she had to spend the evening with Grant's friends, she would know how to be interesting.

Grant came into the room and shut the door behind him. Her heartbeat picked up as it always did whenever he was near. It was nice when they were alone. Knowing he wanted to prevent anyone from interrupting them was all the more thrilling.

"I'm sorry I didn't get to see much of you today," he said as he sat next to her. "I had intended to spend the entire day with you."

"You had to take care of the railway investment. I understand."

"I don't mean to seem uninterested in you."

"I don't think you're not interested in me. You took me and Lucinda to the market this morning. I had a wonderful time."

He accepted the cup she gave him. "Did you?"

She nodded. "It's nice doing things with you and Lucinda. My mother died early. I never got to know her. When we're together, it almost feels like I'm able to get a second chance." Realizing how silly that sounded, she hurried to add, "I mean, I know I'm the mother now. It's not exactly the same thing. I mean, it's…it's…" Unable to find the right words, she blushed. Great. Now she felt like a fool. It was no wonder she was so boring at that dinner party. But even so, it was better to be boring than not make any sense when she was talking.

He put a comforting hand on her knee. "We're a family." He smiled. "It's nice. It makes life complete."

Glad he didn't think she was silly, she relaxed. "You worded that much better than I did."

He chuckled. "There's nothing wrong with the way you worded things."

She rolled her eyes. "Oh, please. I rambled on like I didn't know the English language."

"There are greater faults a lady can have. But truly, I didn't mind. I'd rather know you enjoy your time with me than not hear it."

Though she felt a bit shy, she said, "I do enjoy being with you."

"I enjoy being with you, too."

He hesitated for a moment then kissed her. She hoped he would let his lips linger on hers, but he kept it brief.

"Tell me about your day," he began as he got ready to drink his tea. "What did you do after I went to see Lord Steinbeck?"

She took a sip of her own tea then said, "I spent some time in this room with Lucinda. We drank tea, just like you and I are doing now, and we had a little bit to eat. She made up a story about the doll. We had something to eat and talked about how you're going to spoil us by giving us so many things."

His lips curled up into a smile. "I don't mind spoiling someone who cares about me."

"Well, I don't take your gifts for granted." She took another sip of her tea. "Rachel and Lydia came by. I didn't even know Lydia was back in London. She didn't send a calling card."

He stopped her before she could continue. "Have you received any correspondence lately?"

Her cheeks warmed. He didn't know about Helena, did he? She'd been careful to keep everything quiet about that. She hadn't even told her friends.

"No, I haven't received anything recently," she replied, hoping he didn't detect that she was hoping to receive something soon.

He must never find out her secret. She'd be so embarrassed. What other wife needed lessons on how to make her husband fall in love with her?

"Lydia wanted to surprise me." She intentionally brought the topic back to her friends, praying that it would make him forget about any missives that might be coming for her. "She eloped with Lord Quinton. She wanted to tell me all about it."

Her ploy worked, for he asked, "Isn't that the gentleman who believes in a bunch of superstitions?"

"Yes. I heard he created quite the fuss at the dinner party Horatio hosted a while back."

"If it's the one I attended, it was a trying evening. I've never met someone more insufferable. He spent the entire evening finding fault with everything." He paused. "I suppose now that he's married to your friend, I'll be seeing more of him."

Carol winced. "You don't mind, do you? I was going to mention a dinner party he and Lydia will be inviting us to after I finished telling you about my day."

"What else did you do today?"

Surprised he would worry about that when she'd just told him about Lydia's dinner party, it took her a few moments to organize her thoughts. "Oh, well, after Lydia told Rachel and me about marrying Lord Quinton, she wanted to go shopping for a new wardrobe. She thought it might be fun to get Lucinda something, and since you said I could buy things if I wanted to, I took her. I had to make her leave the room while Lydia told me a few things because the topic was too mature for her."

"What did you talk about?"

Though they were alone, Carol lowered her voice. "Apparently, her brother said something unflattering about a lady, and the lady's brother followed him to the country and tried to kill him." Noting the shock on his face, she added, "I couldn't believe it, either. But Lydia was there when the lady's brother chased him with a sword. In the end, Lydia's brother was able to fend him off, but he had to kill the lady's brother in order to do it. They're back in London now dealing with the ramifications of what happened. Lucinda was upset that I had the maid take her out of the room, but you understand that I couldn't have Lucinda hear all of that."

"Yes, I understand. I wouldn't have wanted her to hear any of that, either."

That was a relief. She was sure he would agree she'd done the right thing, but it was nice to know that for sure. "Anyway, when Lydia was done telling us everything, I asked the maid to bring Lucinda back to the drawing room. That's when we went shopping. I promised her that she could wear the blue frock tomorrow." She paused. "Is it all right that I did that?"

"Of course, it's all right. I want you to feel comfortable in your role as her mother."

"I'm beginning to."

He smiled. "So, did you do anything else today?"

"No. After we went shopping, we came back here. Lucinda fell asleep while Lydia was picking out her last gown."

He took a sip of his tea. "It sounds like you had an enjoyable day."

"I did. Was your day good, too?"

"It seems so."

She didn't know what to make of that response. She'd never heard a simple question answered like that before. Was there something she was missing?

"You mentioned a dinner party with Lord Quinton and your friends?" he asked.

Forcing her attention back to the dinner party, she said, "Since Lydia is back, we thought it might be nice if we could all get together with our husbands. Do you like Rachel's husband?"

"Yes, I think we get along fine."

"If it's any consolation, Rachel and Edwin think Lord Quinton is strange."

He shook his head. "If he acts like he did at Horatio's dinner party, you'll think he's strange, too."

Her primary motive for wanting to go to the dinner party had nothing to do with finding out how strange Lydia's husband was, but she supposed she might find out what Grant and Rachel kept alluding to when the evening came. The important thing was he was willing to go to the dinner party. She was looking forward to it. It'd be nice to attend a dinner where she wasn't such a wallflower. Once she met with Helena, she would learn how to do better when confronted with people she barely knew. She would stay home tomorrow so she didn't miss the lady's missive when it came.

Chapter Twenty-One

Grant walked up to the address printed on the stationary. He was surprised Mr. Weber was in such a nice part of London. Yes, Mr. Weber had been at the ball. He'd been dressed well enough. But Grant wouldn't have thought he'd be living among the wealthiest of the Ton. Perhaps he had a brother whose title availed him to this level of stature in the community. Sometimes it wasn't a gentleman's wealth that put him among the right people. The right connection could do it, too.

Well, whatever Mr. Weber's situation, Grant didn't care. All he wanted was for Mr. Weber to leave Carol alone. After talking to her yesterday, he doubted Carol knew Mr. Weber was trying to contact her. He had seen Carol leave the carriage with Lucinda, and he recognized Lydia and Rachel as they talked. The number of boxes tied to the top of the carriage was enough to let him know they had been shopping, and it made sense that more than one lady could accumulate that much in one afternoon. Also, that morning, Lucinda had worn the frock Carol had bought for her yesterday, and Lucinda had told him how much fun she'd had with Carol.

"Like her?" Lucinda had asked him after Carol had left the room to help Amelia pick out a gown to wear for her stroll through London.

Grant had smiled at Lucinda. "Yes, I like your mother."

"She like you," Lucinda had said.

"How do you know that?" he'd asked.

"She tell me." Then she had turned her attention to the cameo pinned to her frock.

Even now, that part of the conversation he had with his daughter warmed him. He didn't see why Carol would lie to a child.

Grant marched up the steps of the townhouse. He was going to get this matter resolved with Mr. Weber, and he was going to do it once and for all. A gentleman living in this part of town would be afraid of losing the respect of the Ton. Fortunately for Grant, he knew the right people to ruin Mr. Weber's good name. He was hoping it wouldn't come to that, but he would do it if it meant Mr. Weber would finally leave Carol alone.

The door opened, and Grant told the footman he had been asked to see the owner of the residence. He proceeded to show the footman the missive as proof.

Grant thought the footman might show some surprise at seeing the name *Helena* on the missive, but he didn't. He just waved for Grant to come into the entryway. Grant didn't like this. Mr. Weber had done this before. He wondered how many wives had been brought here without realizing the true identity of the person sending out those missives.

"If you'll follow me," the footman began, "I'll take you to the drawing room."

Grant folded the missive and tucked it into his pocket. Once he entered the room, the footman asked him if he wanted something to drink. Grant declined the offer but decided to sit when the footman gestured to the chair.

Grant took a good look around the room. It was decorated as elaborately as he expected before entering the townhouse. The peach furniture was new, and it had elaborate etchings that let Grant know someone had spent a lot of time making it. The curtains were a peach color. The color was an odd one for a bachelor to pick, but if Mr. Weber was used to luring ladies here, Grant supposed this color was for their benefit. There were no portraits on the walls to give the room a personal touch, but the paintings featured pleasant scenes from different places in London.

For all intents and purposes, it was hard to believe this was someone's personal residence. It seemed more like a public room. It was warm but also reserved at the same time. Perhaps Mr. Weber wanted to give the impression he cared for these ladies when all he really intended to do was have his fun with them and then throw them away. If Grant knew anyone at the *Tittletattle*, he would report Mr. Weber at once. That would stop Mr. Weber from seeking out other gentlemen's wives.

Annoyed, Grant jumped to his feet and paced the room. He had worked on a speech he intended to give Mr. Weber, but he didn't think it would be stern enough. This room was just as flippant as Mr. Weber's behavior at the ball.

A lady stepped into the room, and Grant halted in surprise. "Are you Mr. Weber's wife?" he blurted out.

The lady's eyes widened. "No. I'm married to the Duke of Ashbourne. What are you doing here, Lord Wright?"

He frowned. "How do you know who I am? I don't recall meeting you before."

"We haven't met." She paused as if thinking over what she ought to say next.

Was she hiding something? Was Mr. Weber using her to aid him in his adulteries? Irritated, Grant pulled out the missive from his pocket and unfolded it. "You might think this is acceptable, but I don't." He closed the distance between them and showed her the missive. "Exactly what do you and Mr. Weber want with my wife?"

Her gaze scanned the missive then focused on him. "I don't know who Mr. Weber is, so I can't tell you what he wants with your wife. As for me, I am the Duchess of Ashbourne, and your wife sought my services."

"What kind of services?"

The lady blinked. "You haven't heard of me?"

"No. Why? Should I know who you are?" Was London all ablaze with rumors about her? "I don't spend my time seeking idle gossip. I have more important things to do with my time."

"I run a reputable business. That's why I'm well-known. A lot of people employ me to help them." She stared at him expectantly, apparently in an attempt to get him to dig up some memory he should have of when he'd heard of her in the past.

"Unless your services involve finances, I haven't heard of you before."

"Really?" By the expression on her face, he didn't know if she was shocked or upset.

"Really. I've never heard of you before today. Exactly what is the nature of your business?"

After a moment, she went over to the desk.

He followed her. "I demand an answer. What are you doing with my wife? Does it have something to do with Mr. Weber?"

"Like you not knowing about my business, I don't know Mr. Weber." She opened the top drawer of her desk and pulled out a leatherbound journal. "My job is to help ladies and gentlemen find someone to marry, though most of the time, I work with ladies. I am in the business of the heart. I help people find love matches. Your wife is the first person who's come to me seeking advice on how to get her husband to fall in love with her."

He blinked in surprise. "Fall in love with her?"

"Yes. It turns out your wife is head over heels in love with you, but she's worried that she's not interesting enough to appeal to you. She hired me to teach her what she could do to make you fall in love with her." She flipped through the journal and showed him the appointment times and dates when Carol had been at this townhouse. "She signed each time she was here, so you can see for yourself, I'm telling you the truth."

Grant took the journal. Carol worried that he wasn't interested in her? She was coming here to find out what she could do to win his affections? He read the entries in the journal. They included the client's name, the date and time the meeting occurred, the topic of the meeting, and fee paid.

Carol had started seeing the Duchess of Ashbourne shortly after they married. The duchess had marked down the initial meeting and made a couple of notes about teaching Carol the art of flirting. He recalled that day. He'd paid Horatio a visit and came home to find that Amelia had gone shopping alone. There was another entry when the duchess had gone to Lord Worsley's ball to see Carol use her flirting techniques with him. There was an entry the next day where they discussed the ball. He turned the page and found an entry marked for today at two where they were to address Carol's ability to be interesting at dinner parties.

He frowned. "What do dinner parties have to do with me?"

"She wasn't happy about the way she handled things at Lord Steinbeck's dinner party. She's afraid she disappointed you."

"How would she disappoint me?"

"All she wrote in the missive was that she couldn't think of anything to say. She wants me to teach her how to be a better conversationalist around your friends. I assure you that everything she's come to me about has been to make you happy with your marriage. I've never consulted a married lady before. I have to say it was refreshing. It's nice to know someone worries about pleasing the person they're already married to."

Yes, that was nice. In fact, it was better than nice. It was wonderful. He had no idea Carol held him in such high esteem.

His gaze went to the other people the duchess had seen. She had quite a few clients. Lord Cadwalader's niece, Lady

Rhoda, had been here for an initial meeting yesterday at three. He recognized Lady Rhoda because she was related to Lord and Lady Cadwalader, and those two were prominent in London. Before that at two, the duchess had seen Miss Hart regarding her courtship with Lord Bennett. He recognized Lord Bennett because Lord Steinbeck had mentioned him. He was the gentleman who was working on the contract for the railway investment.

If these entries didn't prove the duchess had a reputable business, nothing did. He shut the journal and gave it back to her. "I'm sorry I barged into this townhouse the way I did. I thought someone was luring my wife here for an affair."

"Someone named Mr. Weber?"

He nodded.

She smiled. "For what it's worth, I think it's sweet that you worried about your marriage." She put the journal back into the desk. "I assume that you didn't let Lady Wright see the missive I sent even though I paid the lad extra money to make sure he didn't give it to anyone but her."

"The lad was faithful. I lied and told him my sister was Lady Wright. She took the missive for me."

"Well, since it turns out you love my client and only came here out of fear of losing her, I won't get upset. I will need to send her another missive, though. I don't want her to think I neglected her. I take this job seriously."

"I understand. I won't interfere with your job anymore."

"All right. Another missive will be coming for her within the hour."

"If it's the same lad, I'll have to let my sister take the missive again."

She chuckled. "There's no need for that. I'll send a different one. I have three that I trust to handle correspondence for me."

Feeling more optimistic about the state of his marriage than he'd ever felt while married to Fiona, he bid the duchess a good day then left the townhouse.

Chapter Twenty-Two

Reginald paced the drawing room while Carol, who was on the settee, wept into a handkerchief. "Why don't you just confess to the murder?" he asked. "The doctor found arsenic in the Duke of Augustine's stomach. That's proof enough he didn't commit suicide."

Mr. Weber, who sat in the chair across from her, held his hand up to stop Reginald. "We need to wait until her husband comes home before continuing with this."

"Why should we wait?" Reginald demanded. "A murderer, even one who is a lady, has no rights."

"Everyone has rights until they are found guilty. We have a process to go through." He gave Reginald a pointed look. "You're a suspect in this, too. You ought to appreciate my thoroughness."

"I didn't do it. It had to be her. How is it breaking the law to ask her if she killed His Grace?"

"She said she didn't do it."

"That doesn't mean she's innocent."

"You said you didn't do it, too. That doesn't make you innocent, either." Mr. Weber motioned to the chair next to him. "Sit. We'll have this conversation when her husband gets here."

Though Reginald didn't look happy, he plopped down into the chair. He glared at Carol, so she shifted her gaze away from him.

This whole thing was a nightmare. When she woke up that morning, the last thing she expected was for her uncle and Mr. Weber, who turned out to be a constable, to show up. She wiped her eyes and her cheeks. Had Constable Weber suspected her of murder at the ball? Had he suspected it as far back as the first time she met him at the menagerie? Was it normal for constables to meet someone suspected of a crime before coming into their homes to announce the accusation?

"This is pointless," Reginald told Constable Weber. "Her husband could be gone for hours. If he's taken a mistress, he might not even come home at all tonight."

Constable Weber glanced at the grandfather clock in the corner of the drawing room. "We'll give it another hour then we'll leave him a message."

They were going to stay here for a whole hour? Carol was barely managing to sit still as it was. She didn't know if she could keep sitting here with her uncle staring at her in that intimidating manner of his. While Constable Weber offered her the benefit of the doubt, he had the power to turn her over to the judge. If the judge believed her uncle, she was going to end up at the gallows.

More tears came, and they came even harder as she thought of what she'd heard about those gallows. The crowd looked on and cheered when people were hung. She'd never once thought that one of the people being hung was falsely accused of their crime. Just how horrific was it that someone could be innocent but hung anyway while people celebrated?

And what was she supposed to tell Grant and her friends? Would they even believe her, or would they believe her uncle?

"If she'd just confess, we could be done with it," her uncle muttered.

She could feel the weight of his stare on her, but she refused to look at him. She was innocent. She had a right to maintain that innocence.

"She is a noblewoman," Constable Weber said. "Murderess or not, we will treat her as such. You will not demand that she confess to it, just as I won't demand you confess to it. We will let the proper authorities handle this."

"But that won't be until midsummer."

"Midsummer isn't far off."

Someone approached the open doorway, and they all looked at Grant as he came into the room. Carol would have fainted with relief if she'd thought he could make all of this go away. But he couldn't. No one could prove she was innocent. It was her word against her uncle's, and her uncle was used to getting his way.

"What's going on here?" Grant asked as he marched into the room.

Constable Weber stood up, and her uncle hurried to follow his lead. "Lord Wright," Constable Weber began, "I am a constable. I've been hired by the new Duke of Augustine to investigate a serious crime. The doctor just finished examining the body of the late Duke of Augustine, and he found traces of arsenic in the duke's stomach. His Grace didn't commit suicide. He was murdered. Your wife and her uncle are both suspects."

A long moment passed before Grant said, "I don't believe what I'm hearing."

At first, Carol thought Grant believed she was guilty, but then he directed his gaze to her, and she knew he didn't believe it after all. That made her feel a little better. At least she had his support.

"I keep telling them I didn't do it, but they refuse to believe me," she told Grant.

Grant went to her side and put a comforting hand on her shoulder. "Don't say anything else. You might say something that they'll distort to fit what they want to hear."

"Ah ha!" Reginald pointed at Grant but looked at Constable Weber. "He's complicit in this. He's hiding the truth for her."

"I am doing no such thing," Grant argued. "As her husband, I have a right to intercede in this matter. We were not given sufficient time to deal with these false accusations. My wife is entitled to a jury to determine if there is evidence of this claim you are making. I, for one, find it difficult to believe that a lady can carry a gentleman up into a noose so that it looks like he hung himself, even if he was poisoned first."

"Does arsenic in her old bedchamber count?" Reginald asked with an expectant look.

Grant narrowed his eyes at him. "That could have been put there by someone else."

Constable Weber got between them and gestured for them to stop arguing. "This will go before a jury. The situation isn't perfect. It would have been better if this accusation of murder had been brought to my attention before the body was buried so the jury could investigate the scene of the crime." He shrugged. "But since we're here now, we will deal with the fact that this will be harder to prove."

"You found arsenic in her bedchamber," Reginald explained. "What more can there be to prove she did it?"

Constable Weber straightened his frock coat. "There will be a jury to determine whether or not this will go before the judge at the Midsummer assizes. Lady Wright, you are not allowed to leave London. Do you understand?" His gaze went to Reginald. "The same goes for you."

"Well, I'd feel more comfortable hiring my own constable," Grant said. "Forgive me, Constable Weber, but I need someone I can trust."

Constable Weber retrieved some papers from his pocket. "I can show you my qualifications. It wasn't your wife I was interested in at the ball. I just wanted to get an idea of what kind of person she was. I did the same thing with the Duke of Havre." He gestured to Reginald. "I talked to him a couple of times before telling him he's a murder suspect."

Grant read through the documentation for a few minutes before he handed it back to him. "While I don't want to argue with you, I have every legal right to hire someone I trust."

Constable Weber shrugged. "Do what you feel you must. You're her husband. I would have explained the situation sooner, but I had to wait until I found proof."

"The arsenic was in Carol's bedchamber, not mine," Reginald repeated.

"It's strange that her bedchamber hadn't been cleaned out yet," Grant replied.

"Forgive me for not having time to go through her bedchamber yet," Reginald spat. "I was busy with some business dealings."

"You two can fight on your own time." Constable Weber put his hat on his head. "I'm done for now."

Reginald shot a piercing look at Carol, but she hurried to avert his gaze so she wouldn't throw up. She didn't care for him any more than she cared for the Duke of Augustine. She didn't know which was greater: her fear of them or her hatred of them. She should have known better than to think Reginald was going to leave her alone. He had been so upset by her reluctance to marry the Duke of Augustine that he'd spent many hours berating her for it. *You should be pleased you're marrying a duke, and a wealthy one at that. Why must you look for ways to avoid him?*

To think that all this time, she thought Reginald was biding his time until he could convince her to talk Grant into securing him an invite to one of Lord Steinbeck's dinner parties. He hadn't planned that at all. No. All of this time, he was plotting a way to have her convicted of murder. But why? Because he hated her as much as she hated him?

After Reginald and Mr. Weber left, Grant shut the door.

"I didn't do it, Grant," she said.

He made his way back to her and settled in the settee. "I know," Grant said as he put his arm around her shoulders. "There's no way you could have done it. You're not strong enough to perform a murder that looked like a suicide. If anyone did it, it was your uncle. I meant what I said. I'm going to find a constable to investigate him."

"But I did hate the Duke of Augustine," Carol admitted, her voice soft. "I was relieved when I found out he was dead."

"That doesn't prove anything."

"It proves that I had a reason to kill him. My friends knew I didn't want to marry him. They also knew I was happy to learn he was dead. Won't a jury find that suspicious, especially when Constable Weber said I had arsenic in my old bedchamber?" Worried he might find that condemning, she added, "It had to have been placed there by someone else because I never bought any."

He shushed her and urged her to lean into him. "Carol, you don't have to prove anything to me. I know you're innocent."

While she appreciated his enthusiastic support, she couldn't help but be confused. "How? As far as I can see, I don't know how a jury will absolve me from this accusation." She quickly wiped a couple more tears that sprang to her eyes. "My uncle wanted him alive. He wanted the marriage. He was bound to get a lot of money from the union, and if there's one thing my uncle loves, it's money."

"I know you're innocent because your uncle reminds me of my first wife. I know how those types of people act. I also know what they're capable of doing."

Surprised, she pulled away from him so she could get a good look at his face. Up to now, Grant hadn't told her anything about his first wife. She'd only been able to deduct that marriage from the little Amelia had shared with her. "Did you hate your first wife?"

He paused for a moment then answered, "I did. And I was relieved when she died. I realize how terrible that sounds, but if you knew her the way I did, then you'd understand it's not so terrible after all."

She could see that even saying this little bit about his first wife was difficult for him. It didn't make him happy to admit that he hated her. He would rather say he had loved her but couldn't. How often had she thought the same about the Duke of Augustine? For years, she'd known his first name but never felt comfortable enough to say it, let alone think it.

"I think I understand," Carol softly said. "I didn't care when I learned the Duke of Augustine was dead. I assumed he killed himself to get out of marrying me."

"So you never suspected he was murdered?"

"No. It never occurred to me. He resented the marriage arrangement as much as I did. Our fathers set it up when we were children. Neither one of us had any say in it. I wish they hadn't come up with the arrangement in the first place. It would have spared us all a lot of grief."

"Carol, I know this isn't the ideal time to bring this up, but I'm very happy with you. In fact, I love you."

"You do?" she asked, not sure she heard him right. Yes, this was something she'd wanted more than anything, but could she trust her ears?

He smiled and placed his hand on the small of her back. "I do. I'm very happy with our marriage."

"I love you, too."

He kissed her. "I had planned to tell you how much you mean to me when I came home, though not quite like this. I'm afraid your uncle and Constable Weber put a damper on the moment."

"No, they didn't. I like knowing you love me. It's especially nice after finding out there's going to be a jury deciding if I committed a murder." As terrible as the situation was, it was less so now. And right now, she'd take any relief that she could get.

He kissed her again. "You didn't do it. I don't know why your uncle made the accusation, though I have my suspicions."

When he didn't explain those suspicions, she asked, "What are they?"

"I'd rather not say. Not yet. I want to consult with my own constable first." He patted the small of her back again then rose to his feet. "I have a feeling now that Constable Weber has confronted you and your uncle, he will act fast. I don't want him to get ahead of me."

She stood up and followed him to the door. "You won't have to do anything dangerous, will you?"

He stopped at the door and turned to her. "No, I won't do anything dangerous." He brushed her cheek with his fingers before giving her a lingering kiss.

There was a knock at the door that startled both of them. He quickly recovered and opened it.

The footman directed his gaze to her. "Lady Wright, a lad is at the door. He says he must deliver a missive directly to you."

A missive? Oh, right! Helena must have sent it. She glanced at Grant, wondering if he would ask about it, but he didn't. She cleared her throat. "I'll be there in a moment."

Grant gave her arm a comforting pat and said, "Don't fret. Your uncle won't get away with this. I'll make sure of it. I need to retrieve something from the library. Then I'll be on my way." He excused himself and left the drawing room.

She watched Grant stride down the hallway. His shoulders were pushed back. His gaze was focused on the path in front of him. He was a gentleman on a mission. No one would guess he had been so sweet and tender with her moments ago. It was no wonder Amelia had accused him of not having any feelings. Carol knew very well he did, but he had the remarkable ability to hide them. That just might give her an advantage in this situation. While her uncle tried to believe he was strong, he couldn't mask his emotions like Grant could. Already, she felt better.

She waited until Grant was out of sight before she went to the front door. The lad gave her the missive then was on his way. She waited until she was back in the drawing room before reading it. As she'd suspected, it was from Helena. Helena apologized for taking so long in getting back to her. Then she wrote that she could come by tomorrow afternoon at one. *Since I didn't get this missive to you sooner, tomorrow's visit will be free,* Helena concluded.

Well, that was nice of her. It was no wonder Carol had heard so many wonderful things about her. Helena might be running a business, but she cared about her clients, too. Best of all, however, was the fact that the lady's advice worked. Those seeking her services didn't do so in vain. Carol now knew for certain that Grant loved her. Because of that, she had no doubt he was going to do whatever it took to prove her innocence.

Chapter Twenty-Three

An hour later, Grant was sitting in his friend's townhouse.

Adam Page, the Earl of Dayton, sipped his tea then settled back in his chair. "This is an unusual request you're making of me, Grant. I've never pretended to be a constable before."

Grant figured Adam wasn't going to be easy, but there wasn't anyone else he trusted to help him with Carol's situation. "You're a good actor. You're better than those people who act at the theatre."

"What I do isn't the same thing they do."

"I didn't say it was the same. They do things for entertainment. You play a part to help people with their problems. My wife has been accused of murder. What problem could be worse than that?"

Adam took another sip of his tea then tapped the edge of the chair's arm.

Grant held his tongue. He couldn't expect Adam to say yes right away, even when offered a lot of money. Ever since Grant had met him, Adam had been careful about the jobs he accepted. And that was part of what made him so good at what he did. He had to genuinely want to play the role.

"How can you be sure your wife didn't commit the crime?" Adam asked. "Ladies have been known to poison people. There was a trial brought before the assizes six years ago where a titled gentleman's mistress poisoned his wife in hopes of marrying him. It didn't take much to prove her guilt in the matter."

Grant shook his head. "Carol's not the type of lady who'd do such a thing."

"And you know that because…?" Adam waited expectantly for his answer.

"Because she's faithful to me in the marriage. In my experience, when someone is honest in one area, they are honest in other areas as well. Besides, I don't see how she could have physically done it. How could a lady hang a dead gentleman?"

"She could have wrapped the noose around his neck and used a pulley to lift him up."

Grant hadn't thought of that. Adam made a good point. He bet Constable Weber had already factored that excuse into the equation.

"This is why I want to hire you," Grant told Adam. "Your knowledge is unmatched by anyone else. You see things that other people miss. You were the one who warned me about Fiona's infidelity."

Adam winced. "There wasn't much to figure out with her. She had a way of looking at other gentlemen that indicated she had a wandering eye."

"That's exactly the kind of insight I need. I think Carol's uncle poisoned the Duke of Augustine. Carol and her uncle don't get along. They put on a pretense of liking each other in public, but there's a tension you can feel between them. It reminds me of how I used to feel when Fiona was alive."

"Not getting along with someone isn't enough to accuse them of murder."

"No, but since Constable Weber found out the duke didn't commit suicide, he would want to have her convicted of the crime in order to save himself."

Adam's eyes lit up. "Yes, that's true." After a moment, he asked, "Given what happened with Fiona, would you have hung yourself to get out of marrying her?"

Grant settled back in his chair and thought over the question. The experience he'd been through with Fiona had been painful. Losing his entire estate would have been less humiliating. But he couldn't see wanting to die because of it. "No, I wouldn't have hung myself. If anything, I would have left the country to start a new life." He gasped and sat up straight in the chair. "Maybe the Duke of Augustine was planning to leave England. Maybe Reginald killed the duke out of spite. From what I heard, the duke had a lot of money."

Adam's eyes widened. "More money than you have?"

Grant nodded. "An uncle who stood to get some of that money would be angry if the duke ran off to avoid marrying his niece." Grant leaned forward in the chair. "We have to act fast. We need to think of a way to mislead her uncle into confessing to the crime. He needs to believe you're a constable. He won't believe me if you're not there."

Adam hesitated for a moment. "How can you be sure you can make him confess? Wasn't he just trying to get Carol to confess?"

"Yes, but she's innocent. It's harder to coax an innocent person into getting a confession. It's a lot easier to get someone who is guilty to do it. Even if they pretend their sin doesn't bother them, deep down, they know what they did was wrong."

"You seem awfully confident you can get this to work."

"I am."

Grant had been able to get Fiona to admit to having multiple affairs. Then he'd gotten her to tell him who fathered Lucinda. At first, Fiona had been determined to protect the cook, but by slipping in the suggestion he'd already talked to the father of the child, she'd finally broken down and confessed. Carol's uncle would be more difficult. Murder was much more serious than an illicit affair. But he was confident that, given the right story and the right details, he could put this whole thing to rest before the day was up.

"I'll think of what we need to say while you make yourself look like a constable," Grant added.

Adam indicated his agreement then left the room.

***

Two hours later, Grant and Adam were ready to confront Carol's uncle. Adam had donned a fake black beard with a matching wig. Then he had given himself padding to look plump. The final touch to this particular disguise was the monocle he wore. Then he put on a coat often worn by the middle class.

They had practiced what they were going to do and say. They would only get one chance at this before the matter went before a jury. Grant had no doubts about Carol's innocence, but he didn't want to put her through the turmoil of having this thing put before a jury and a possible trial. And then there would be the rumors people would make up to satisfy their morbid need for gossip. There was no telling what sort of stories they'd come up with about her.

Word was currently going around London about an unmarried lady who'd recently been accused of sharing dalliances with anyone who wore breeches. Grant had overheard someone snickering about it at the most recent ball. Though he had admonished the person to spend his time on better things, he doubted the person would listen. Once a rumor took hold, it was impossible to contain it. He would not let people snicker about Carol the same way they snickered about that poor lady.

"You do realize this might not work," Adam told him as the carriage took them to Reginald's townhouse.

"I realize that, but there's also a chance it might. I owe it to Carol to try."

Adam studied him for a moment. "Why do I get the impression you've done something like this before?"

Grant chose not to respond. Instead, he turned his gaze to the window. Adam was Fiona's second cousin. While he'd been in attendance at the wedding, he hadn't cared for her all that much. He'd been there because a lot of her family wanted to be there. As soon as Grant met him, he liked him. The two became friends from there. And though Grant saw him from time to time, Adam's work kept him busy.

Grant looked back at him. "Thank you for doing this. To be honest, I wasn't sure you'd be available today."

Adam shrugged but smiled. "You happened to come with your request while I was between jobs."

"You don't do this kind of thing for the money. You enjoy it."

"Yes, but the money is nice. I have to earn money somehow, and I'd rather do it while having fun. I don't like sitting around discussing all of those investments like you."

"I know." Which was why Grant hadn't bothered to invite him to Lord Steinbeck's dinner party. "I should introduce you to Carol. I think you'd like her. She's nothing like Fiona." The carriage came to a stop, and Grant's attention went back to the matter at hand. "Do you have your voice for the constable ready?"

Adam repeated the phrase, "I am Constable Penquite," several times in various pitches. Once he found the one he liked, he nodded.

Grant opened the door of the carriage. He could have waited for the footman to open it, but doing it himself helped to convey a sense of purpose. If Carol's uncle happened to see him from one of the windows, he wanted her uncle to pick up on that purpose. Any time someone hesitated to do anything, it was a sign of uncertainty. He had brought Adam here to play a part, but he was playing a part, too.

The two marched up the steps of the townhouse. Since Adam was the constable, Grant let him knock on the door.

"You really believe your wife is innocent," Adam whispered. "For your sake, I hope you're right."

Grant's eyebrows furrowed. He hadn't realized Adam had doubts about what he was doing. If Adam felt that way, why did he agree to do this?

The answer was simple, of course. Adam was his friend. And all Grant was asking was for Adam to help him prove her innocence. Grant wasn't asking Adam to help her flee London. If Grant had asked him to do that, Adam would have said no.

The front door opened.

"Pardon us for coming by unannounced, but I am Constable Penquite. I need to speak to the Duke of Havre."

"I'm afraid His Grace isn't here at the moment," the footman said.

"That's quite all right. We don't mind waiting." Adam stepped into the entryway, and Grant hurried to follow him. "The situation is serious. I must talk to him as soon as he comes home. It can't wait until tomorrow."

The footman looked baffled but shut the door then led them to a drawing room. "I don't know when His Grace will return. He didn't tell me."

"That's all right," Adam said. "We're patient gentlemen." Adam glanced over at Grant as if asking him if he was willing to commit to waiting for hours.

Grant would wait here for years if it meant he could prove Carol was innocent. A lady who went through all the trouble of hiring the Duchess of Ashbourne to teach her how to make him fall in love with her deserved his best. "I have nowhere I need to be," Grant replied. "I can stay here all night if necessary. Though," he added with a glance at the footman, "I will want to send my wife a note if I am delayed for longer than a couple of hours."

The footman still seemed overwhelmed but allowed them to enter the drawing room. After an awkward moment, he asked them, "Would you like something to eat or drink?"

"We'll have your best brandy and scones," Adam said before Grant could answer. Then he sat down, crossed his legs, folded his hands, and set them in his lap.

Grant supposed sitting was the best thing to do. It would show the footman that they were determined not to move anywhere, just in case the footman went to get the butler to throw them out. Not all servants were as timid as this one. He settled in the chair across from Adam then gave the footman an expectant look.

The footman jerked then rushed out of the room.

Grant released his breath.

Adam unfolded his hands, uncrossed his legs, and scooted to the edge of his chair. "I'll keep watch at the door," he whispered. "When he returns, I'll wave my hand and come back to this chair."

Grant nodded. This was a prime opportunity. Something in this room might give him a clue. Grant jumped to his feet and started to inspect the room.

Chapter Twenty-Four

Carol couldn't relax enough to focus on what Amelia was telling her. She hadn't told Amelia about being accused of murder. Thinking of it was too awful. If she started talking about it, she'd end up crying all over again.

"I haven't told Reuben that I'm no longer seeing my other suitors," Amelia rambled as she poured more tea into her cup. "I thought I might tell him when I saw him earlier today, but then I decided against it." She shrugged and set the teapot back on the tray. "I suppose Grant is right to be careful. Even if it's not right to keep suitors I have no interest in, it's probably not wise to let Reuben know he's the only suitor I have." She picked up her cup and sipped the tea. "Besides, this way, I look more attractive because he thinks other gentlemen desire me. At least, I hope I look more attractive to Reuben. What do you think?"

Carol forced her attention to the conversation. Since she'd been able to pick up on half of what Amelia was saying, she was able to make a suitable reply. "I never had to worry about attracting suitors like you do, but I have noticed that ladies who already have suitors seem to attract more."

Quite frankly, Carol had never made any sense of it. One would think gentlemen would focus their efforts on ladies who didn't have any suitors. If she was a gentleman, that's what she would do. But then, she never did care for competition. Maybe gentlemen preferred having to compete with other gentlemen to win the hand of a lady.

Amelia sipped her tea. "In that case, it's a good thing I didn't tell Reuben he's my only suitor. Things are going so well between us. I don't want to ruin it."

"So you're really that confident he's going to marry you?"

"There are little things he says that make me think he will. Last week, he asked me what I'd like to name my future children. Today, he asked me what color drapes and furnishing I like."

Carol blinked in surprise. "He came out and asked you those questions?"

Amelia nodded. "Sometimes he even talks about taking me to his family's estate so he can show me where he liked to fish while growing up."

"If he's talking like that, I can see why you think a proposal is imminent. If a gentleman was doing that with me, I'd tell my other suitors I wasn't interested in them, too."

"That's why I did it. I'm just glad Grant finally came around to accepting it. I expected an awful fight when I told him what I did." She glanced at the doorway. "Speaking of my brother, how long will he be out?"

At the reminder of why Grant had left earlier that day, Carol also glanced at the doorway. "I don't know."

"It's not like him to be out this late without saying something. The maid will be done getting Lucinda ready for dinner."

Carol resisted the urge to respond. For a brief moment, while Amelia was explaining how she knew Reuben was going to propose to her, she had forgotten her own problems. It'd been nice to think of something else for a change. Wishing to get back to that, she asked, "What kind of wedding will you and Reuben have?"

"I think we'll have a formal one with the banns, a ceremony, and a wedding breakfast. It's not like when you and Grant married. Because of the situation with the Duke of

Augustine, Grant felt it best to keep the wedding quiet so as not to encourage gossip."

"Yes, the news about the Duke of Augustine was terrible." And it would get more terrible once word spread that she had been accused of murdering him.

The knot in Carol's stomach tightened. How was she supposed to eat dinner? How was she supposed to eat breakfast? How was she supposed to eat at all? She didn't even know if she could sleep tonight.

"I think I'll have a blue gown made for the wedding," Amelia said, her tone taking on a wistful quality. "I might even wear the cameo that was pinned to my gown the evening we met. I think wearing it on our wedding day might be a nice touch."

Fortunately, Amelia kept talking, which afforded Carol a reprieve from having to respond. Carol didn't know how much more she could keep up with her part in this conversation. She glanced at the doorway again. Grant seemed confident he could prove her innocence. She had no idea what he had in mind when he went to find a constable. It didn't seem like there was anything the constable could do, but Grant was so confident that she couldn't help but hope he would be successful in this venture.

***

It was nearing ten in the evening. Grant had exhausted every possible hiding place in the drawing room where Reginald might have hidden something. He hadn't come up with anything conclusive, but he had found a schedule of dates and times for passenger ships. The schedule had been tucked away in the back of the top drawer in the desk. Upon first glance, Grant almost missed it. It was only going through the drawer a second time that he saw it.

At first, he and Adam thought Reginald was planning to leave England, but then they realized the dates had already passed. Reginald was still in London. He wasn't using this schedule for himself. But the schedule was there for a reason. Without having anything else to use, they concluded the dates and the fact that the passenger ships were all going to America had to be important to Reginald. From there, they planned on how they were going to use the schedule when confronting Reginald. Grant shifted in the chair as he ran the dates over in his mind. The dates had to be significant. But how?

He glanced over at Adam, who drummed his fingers on the arms of his chair. "Thank you for staying here."

Adam offered a shrug. "I had nothing better to do this evening."

Grant was sure Adam could have come up with something far more entertaining to do than sit in a drawing room watching the walls, but it was nice of him to lie for his sake.

They sat in silence for another few minutes before they heard footsteps approaching the drawing room. They straightened up in their chairs. As Grant hoped, Reginald was finally here.

"They insisted the matter was urgent," the footman was telling him. "That right there is Constable Penquite." He gestured to Adam. "And that is Lord Wright."

Grant could tell Reginald wasn't happy to see either one of them, but Reginald allowed the footman to go without an argument. Grant and Adam rose to their feet. Reginald hadn't given Carol any warning he was going to barge in on her with a constable. It was nice to be able to startle him the same way he had startled her.

"I see you are a man of your word," Reginald said as he shut the door. "Is this gentleman really a constable?"

"Of course, he is," Grant replied. "Do I look like someone who would bring in a gentleman who was pretending to be a constable?"

Reginald eyed him for a moment then walked over to Adam. "I would like to see proof that you are a constable. Grant didn't believe Constable Weber. I don't believe you."

Adam obliged the gentleman by showing him the papers he and Grant had carefully drafted up.

After a moment, Reginald let out a sigh. "All right, Grant. Do you really think you can absolve Carol from guilt by accusing me of murder?"

"I wouldn't have come here if I didn't." Grant took a step around Reginald so he had to turn his back to Adam. "Unlike Constable Weber, Constable Penquite actually found something that points you to the duke's murder."

Reginald snorted. "And you were able to come up with this in a few hours?"

Grant gestured to Adam. "Talk to him for yourself."

Reginald turned back to Adam so that his back was to Grant. "What proof did you come up with?"

Grant offered Adam a nod to let him know it was time to start in on the questions they had rehearsed.

"It's a nice time of year to travel, don't you think?" Adam asked Reginald.

Grant watched Reginald jerk back in surprise. "What does that have to do with the duke?"

Something in Reginald's tone as he spoke the words "the duke" hinted that Reginald was angry at the gentleman. Grant signaled to Adam to ask the fourth question they had practiced while they waited for Reginald to arrive.

"Before coming here, we made an inquiry with the Duke of Augustine's staff. The new one decided to retain all of the servants. That made my job quick." Adam paused. "Did you know the steward recorded the duke's plans for traveling a few weeks ago?"

Grant noted the way Reginald's hand twitched.

"I fail to see what this has to do with the murder," Reginald said. "People travel all the time."

Grant signaled for Adam to ask the second question they had rehearsed.

"But why travel right before a marriage?" Adam asked.

"Yes," Grant interjected. "That's what I'm wondering, too. Wasn't Carol supposed to marry the duke at that time?"

A flicker of apprehension crossed Reginald's face.

Grant glanced at Adam. So there was a connection between the Duke of Augustine and that shipping schedule they found in Reginald's desk. Maybe with a little more prodding, he and Adam might get more information.

"The butler mentioned having to pack the duke's things," Grant said.

"You two had the time to ask the duke's servants questions before coming here?" Reginald snapped.

"Of course, we did," Adam spoke up. "That's what a good constable does. It's the correct procedure for cases like this. I can't help it if Constable Weber was negligent in this area."

Grant wasn't sure if Constable Weber asked those servants questions or not, but they had a slight advantage over Reginald since he believed Adam had talked to the duke's staff. Grant had to follow his hunch. He'd done it with Fiona, and it worked. It might work this time as well.

"We found out that the duke's traveling dates coincided with the time he was supposed to marry Carol," Grant inserted.

Reginald glowered at him.

"That upsets you," Grant said, surprised that Reginald should care whether or not the duke left England. "You really wanted that marriage to take place between the duke and Carol."

Reginald's face grew red, but his tone calmed in an effort to show restraint. "It was an arranged marriage. The Duke of Augustine had a duty to go through with it."

Ah, so that was it. Reginald had found out the duke planned to leave the country to avoid marrying Carol, and it had made him furious. Perhaps, he was so furious that he murdered the duke. But Grant wagered Reginald hadn't been upset for Carol's sake. No gentleman murdered another gentleman over something like that. They might, however, kill someone over money. A lot of money was exchanged when a marriage took place. Grant hadn't been able to take a look at Reginald's ledger, but if he did, he bet it revealed a lot of debt.

"It's a shame you weren't nicer to Carol, Your Grace," Grant said, choosing his words with great care. "If you had been, I would have asked Lord Steinbeck to invite you to the dinner party that I attended the other night."

Reginald's face turned a deeper shade of red.

It was as he suspected. Money was the motive. "The Duke of Augustine was far wealthier than I am," Grant continued. "He could have easily gone to another country to start a new life." He paused. "In America, no one could make him come back here to marry her." His gaze went to Adam, knowing Adam would pick up on the hint to continue.

Adam stepped closer to Reginald. "We found a ticket for a passenger ship heading to America in the duke's residence. I'm sure the jury will be interested in that when they investigate the murder."

Grant hurried to jump in before Reginald could say anything. It was best to keep talking so that Reginald didn't have time to think. Thinking would only allow him time to lie. "The jury will be especially interested when the maid in your townhouse tells them she saw you put the arsenic bottle in Carol's old bedchamber."

Reginald swung back to face Grant. "You interviewed my servants, too?"

Was that a confession, or was it a question spoken in shock? Grant decided to respond as if Reginald was guilty. "My constable doesn't need to ask a lot of questions to piece everything together."

Reginald squirmed.

"She saw you do it, and she's willing to testify since we promised to keep her safe at my residence," Grant added.

"The maid is a young twit," Reginald blurted out. "Who will believe her?"

"The judge will believe her," Adam replied. "A servant's word, even one who is young and female, can offer evidence."

"That still doesn't mean anything," Reginald argued. "Servants can lie. The maid doesn't like me. She always preferred Carol. She could be lying to protect her. We need to stick with the facts, things we can know without any doubt."

Reginald was speaking faster than he was thinking now. Fiona had done just the same thing before breaking down and telling him the cook was Lucinda's father.

"We know that the Duke of Augustine was going to leave England," Grant interrupted.

"He had no right to leave!"

"But he wanted to, and you couldn't handle it," Grant said.

"The marriage was arranged," Reginald shot back. "Other gentlemen don't run from their responsibilities, but he did. He deserved to die."

Grant noted the surprised expression on Adam's face and knew they were close to getting Reginald to admit to committing the murder. "Why involve Carol in this?" Grant pressed. "She didn't plan to leave in order to avoid the marriage."

"She was the reason he wanted to leave!" Reginald yelled.

Grant's gaze went to Adam. As far as he was concerned that was an admission of guilt, but he needed someone Reginald believed to be a constable to secure the confession.

"You hate your niece, don't you?" Adam asked.

Reginald turned back to Adam. "She hates me as much as I hate her. It's no secret we hate each other."

Grant gestured for Adam to use the seventh question they had rehearsed.

"Everything we found tonight points you to the crime," Adam said. "Why don't you just confess? Why drag this out in court?"

Reginald shook. "It wasn't my intention for anyone to find arsenic in the duke's stomach. Carol and I don't have to go through any of this." Reginald gasped, as if realizing he had said too much. He grew quiet.

Adam went over to Grant so that Reginald had to look at him. "So you did murder the Duke of Augustine."

Reginald looked as if he was going to argue his innocence for a moment. If he chose to do that, there was nothing Grant could do about it. Neither he nor Adam had any proof. They hadn't spoken to the Duke of Augustine's staff. They hadn't spoken to the maid of this household. They didn't know if the duke had purchased a ticket to leave England. All they had was a piece of paper with dates and ships heading for America. This was one big gamble. But Grant maintained his focus on Reginald as if they did have proof, and Adam, being the actor he was, did the same.

Finally, after what seemed like forever, Reginald let out a heavy sigh. "Yes, I did it. I was angry. I found out that he was going to leave England and poisoned him. Then I panicked and made it look like he hung himself. If his cousin hadn't hired Constable Weber, no one would have been the wiser. We could have all gone on believing he killed himself."

Adam offered a satisfied nod, and Grant relaxed. Good. They had done it. They had managed to get to the truth of the situation. Carol wouldn't have to be dragged through an agonizing trial just to prove she was innocent.

"Since there's no doubt you murdered the Duke of Augustine," Adam quietly began, "we will arrange for you to go to jail where the judge will decide your fate."

Head bowed, Reginald didn't protest as they led him out of the townhouse.

Chapter Twenty-Five

Carol sat in the entryway by the door. The clock had chimed two in the morning not more than five minutes ago. She had relieved the footman of his duties at ten o'clock. She couldn't sleep, nor could she read to help pass the time. She wasn't going to feel better until Grant returned. That was, if he returned. The knot in her stomach twisted, and she had to fight back the swell of nausea that rose up in her throat.

When Grant left, he said he was going to get a constable. He'd even added that he knew just the right person for the job. If he'd already had someone in mind, then it shouldn't have taken him this long to return home. He must have run into some sort of trouble, and try as she might, she couldn't get the image of her uncle out of her mind. If her uncle murdered the Duke of Augustine, which it seemed he must have done since she knew she didn't do it, then who knew if her uncle would murder Grant?

She took a deep breath in an effort to calm herself. It didn't work. She couldn't relax. She wasn't superstitious by nature, but it almost seemed like things had been going too well for her. She should have expected something bad to happen.

She stood up and paced the floor. No, she couldn't think this way. She needed to have hope. Thinking the worst wasn't going to do her any good.

She caught sight of a carriage coming down the street and ran to the door. It was Grant's carriage! She held her breath and waited as it came to a stop. Grant stepped out of it. He was still alive!

Without thinking, she opened the door and ran down the steps to hug him. "I worried when you didn't come home earlier."

He hugged her in return. "It's nice to know you missed me."

"I did miss you, but I was also afraid my uncle did something to you."

He pulled away from her, slipped his arm around her waist, and led her back up the steps. "I have good news, and I'm glad I can share it with you tonight. Your uncle confessed to the murder. He is now in jail."

Sure she hadn't heard right, she asked, "What did you say?"

He waited until they were inside the townhouse before he answered her. "I took a risk, and it paid off. Your uncle confessed to the murder. He not only confessed it to me, but he confessed it to the authorities as well. I can't do much about the gossip that is due to erupt once word gets out that he murdered the duke, but I was able to stop any rumors that you were accused of the crime. Your reputation won't be tarnished because of this incident."

Her reputation had been the least of her worries. In fact, she hadn't once even bothered to think of what all of this might mean for what people would say about her. But now she realized Grant was right. Even if she was innocent, her reputation could have suffered.

She hugged him again. "I can't believe you went through all of this trouble for me."

He kissed her. "I'd do anything for you, Carol. Your love means everything to me."

She smiled. "Amelia was wrong about you when she said you don't have feelings. You care very deeply for those you love. I'm very lucky that you love me. Before I met you, I had no idea love could be this wonderful. Now I understand why one of my friends eloped with the butler and the other eloped with a gentleman prone to superstition."

He chuckled. "Well, I'm not sure about the friend who ran off with the gentleman prone to superstition. To my dying day, I'll never understand why she wanted to marry him. But because she wanted him, it meant you and I could be together, and for that, I'm grateful Lord Quinton insisted on changing partners at Horatio's dinner party."

Her skin tingled in excitement. She might never get tired of hearing him confess his feelings for her. She was tempted to ask him to tell her all of this again but realized more sentiment would come in due time. For the moment, she was just happy he was all right and that they were going to be able to spend the rest of their lives together because the Duke of Augustine's murder had been put to rest.

"I love you, Grant," she whispered.

He smiled then gave her another kiss, and this time, he didn't end it right away. He let his lips linger on hers for a delightfully long time. Her heartbeat picked up in excitement. While she didn't have to worry about her uncle anymore, all of this kissing was giving her another reason to delay sleep.

"Do you want to continue this upstairs?" she asked when the kiss ended.

"I was about to ask you the same thing," came his husky reply.

Without another word, he led her to her bedchamber.

***

The next morning, Carol and Grant slept in late. She usually had dreams while sleeping, but she didn't recall any as she woke up. Within seconds, the memories from the day before came back to her. She jerked then recalled that everything turned out all right. She breathed a sigh of relief.

"I hope that jerk you just gave wasn't because I'm in your bed."

Noting the teasing tone in Grant's voice, her gaze went to him. She put her hand over her heart. "It took me a moment to remember how everything turned out yesterday."

He shifted closer to her and pulled her into his arms. "Your uncle is tucked away in jail where he belongs. If you don't believe me, I'm sure it'll be in the *Tittletattle* within a week."

She snuggled up to him. "I believe you. I can't believe my uncle murdered the Duke of Augustine."

"Anger can make people do unimaginable things. Not everyone knows how to deal with their emotions properly." He brushed her cheek with his fingers. "Try not to think about it. It does no good to dwell on unpleasant things."

He was right. She would be better off focusing on the future. After spending so much time with her uncle and battling her apprehension about marrying the Duke of Augustine, Grant was a refreshing change. "It's a shame that more gentlemen aren't like you. The world would be a better place if they were."

"Instead of telling me that, why don't you show me?"

Again, his voice had taken on a teasing tone. With a smile, she wrapped her arms around his neck and kissed him. The kiss started off light, as it always did, but before long, the urge to do more swept over her. In the past, Grant had initiated a deeper level of intimacy. Perhaps she ought to be the one to do it this time.

She parted her lips in silent encouragement to deepen the kiss. He obeyed her leading, and their tongues began to interlace in earnest. His hand slid down to her breast, and he cupped it in his hand. Up to now, she hadn't dared to explore him. Yes, she'd seen him naked. She'd marked the differences between them. But she hadn't dared touch him down there.

Since she enjoyed it when he touched her in her most intimate places, she thought he might like it if she did the same to him. Besides, she was safe with him. He loved her. Pushing past a bout of shyness, she reached between them and touched his erection. He let out a moan that let her know he enjoyed her touch. He shifted his hips so his penis was more fully in her palm. Feeling bolder, she cupped him in her hand with one hand and traced the tip with her free hand.

"That feels good," he murmured then kissed her again, this time in greater urgency.

She didn't realize how thrilling it would be to touch him like this, nor did she realize how much it would excite him.

He slid partly out of her hand and then slid all the way back in. He repeated this action several times before he slid his fingers into her. She parted her legs farther and took him deeper into her. The mutual giving of pleasure was as stimulating as it was sweet. It was just like him to insist on taking care of her while she took care of him. She was certain not every husband loved his wife this way. He was a very considerate lover.

His mouth left hers and traveled down her neck and then down to her breasts. He spent time kissing them. He even brushed his tongue over her nipples in a way that made her core ache. Had his fingers not been stroking her in the most pleasant way, she didn't know if she could handle the tension.

She brought her hands up to his shoulders and squeezed them. He left a trail of kisses to where his fingers were. She groaned in anticipation. She knew what he was going to do, and she couldn't wait. Every time he made love to her this way, her body felt as if it were on fire. All she could think about was how good everything felt. She didn't just want him. She needed him.

He proceeded to caress her nub with his tongue. She murmured his name and lifted her hips to better accommodate him. She could never hold back her excitement when he made love to her this way. The ache building up deep inside her prompted her to let him know exactly how much she wanted him to continue. She cried out again, this time louder than before, and gripped the sheets. The tension continued to build up within her until she thought she couldn't take it anymore. Finally, her core burst, and she found her release. Wave after wave of pleasure swept over her. After the waves ebbed, he shifted so that he could enter her.

She was so wet that he slid in with no effort. Groaning, he pulled slightly out of her and then went back in. He repeated the action again and again. Though weak, she held him close to her and guided him along. He stilled a few times, his body tense, and he waited for several long moments before he resumed his thrusting. He was delaying his climax, and she couldn't blame him. The journey was exquisite in its own right. But after several times of doing this, he finally gave in to the need for release and climaxed. He cried out her name and stilled.

When he collapsed in her arms, she pressed her cheek to his. No one would guess it to look at him, but he was a very passionate lover. After his heartbeat calmed, he spent time kissing her. She liked that he remained inside her while doing so. Though satisfied, their bodies were still entwined. She had no way of knowing how long they were kissing before he slid out of her and drew her into his arms.

"What do you want to do today?" he asked as he kissed her temple.

"If it was up to me, I'd stay here all day with you," she admitted, her voice quiet as she made her confession. "But I have a feeling we ought to tell Amelia what happened before she finds out from someone else. And it would be nice to do something with Lucinda. I like it when we do things together as a family."

He squeezed her shoulders. "I like that, too. I did well when I married you." He gave her another kiss. "All right, I'll have baths brought up for us. Then we'll get something to eat and go out. I have a feeling Amelia will want to talk about Reuben. To stop her from boring us, why don't we take Lucinda to the circus?"

"I thought you liked Reuben."

"I do, but there's only so much I want to hear about him. You can't tell me that you haven't noticed everything she talks about lately is about Reuben."

"Yes, I have noticed that."

"Do you want to spend the entire day hearing about him?"

"You made your point. No, I don't." Recalling the time she was supposed to meet Helena, she sat up. "I just remembered that I have to see a friend at one today. Can we take Lucinda to the circus at two?"

"Of course, we can." He sat up then glanced at her breasts. "If we don't get out of bed right now, I'll be tempted to keep you here all day. I might be patient, but even I have my limitations." He hurried to get out of the bed and slipped on his robe.

Carol hid her smile. It was rather nice to know that in addition to Grant loving her, he also desired her. She couldn't wait to thank Helena for her help. She slipped out of the bed as he pulled the cord to summon the maid to get started on their baths.

Chapter Twenty-Six

"I can't thank you enough for your assistance," Carol told Helena later that day as she entered the duchess' drawing room. "I know without any doubt that my husband loves me. He expressed his feelings for me yesterday."

Helena hugged her. "I'm glad. It was a refreshing change to take on this task. I'm so used to helping people find someone to marry. I hope I can take on other clients who would like to make their marriages love matches."

"Your methods work. I'll recommend you to anyone who might be in the same situation I was. A lot of marriages are arranged or done out of duty."

"I wish that every marriage could be a love match. Things would be much better if they were." Helena paused then added, "I have something to give you that I think your husband will like." She headed for the desk.

Carol's eyebrows furrowed as she followed her. "What is it?"

Helena opened a drawer and pulled out a silky pink ribbon. "It's a favor. In medieval times, a lady would give a knight a token of her affection. This token was called a favor. He could carry it with him as a reminder of her love for him. Since your husband loves you, I think he would enjoy having a symbol of your love for him. I want you to take this and dip it in your favorite perfume. Then give it to him."

Surprised, Carol accepted the pretty ribbon. "Do you really think he'll like this?"

Helena nodded. "I do. The nice thing about the ribbon is that it's discreet. He can put it in his pocket and carry it around with him during the day. Even when you aren't with him, he'll have a sweet reminder of you."

Carol smiled as she studied the ribbon. Helena had chosen a fabric that would, undoubtedly, last for many years. It had to be expensive. "How much do I owe you for it?"

"It's a gift. You don't owe me anything."

"But you spent a lot of money on it, and you're not charging me for today's visit."

Helena shrugged. "I have more than enough money. My business continues to flourish, and my husband has made some sound financial investments. Besides, it makes me happy to know a marriage is doing well."

Carol was ready to insist she pay the lady, but then she thought better of it. Helena wouldn't have given this as a gift if she didn't want to. The best way Carol could honor that gift was by accepting it. "Thank you. It's lovely. I can't wait to give it to him."

"Remember to dip in your favorite perfume first. You just need a small amount of it."

"I will. I promise." Excited, Carol wished her a good day, thanked her again, and headed for home.

***

"Don't feel bad about the way things went between me and Amelia," Horatio told Grant as they sipped brandy in Grant's drawing room.

Grant handed Lucinda a scone so she wouldn't get bored while he and Horatio talked. He had promised to have Lucinda ready by the time Carol came back so they could head out to the circus. The impromptu visit from Horatio hadn't been planned, but it was nice to have the distraction so he didn't miss Carol too much.

"I wish Amelia would give you a chance to court her," Grant told him, "but she is determined that if she doesn't marry Mr. St. George, she will not marry anyone. It's a foolish decision. I have tried to reason with her, but she refuses to listen to me. What if things don't work out with him? What will she do then?"

Horatio sipped his tea. "If there is no one else she wants, then it'll probably be better if she never marries."

"I don't know. Spinsterhood isn't something I want for her. I want her to have love. I want her to have a husband and children. I want her life to be complete." Grant was fortunate enough to experience such fulfillment. It would be a shame if Amelia didn't.

"I know it's not a socially approved opinion, but some people don't need to marry in order to feel complete. They are complete already with their family, their friends, their work, and their interests. Sometimes a title can feel like a burden because society says you must have a son. If it was up to me, I'd leave the title to my cousin and be done with it. To be honest, I wasn't all that disappointed when Amelia told me she didn't want me to be her suitor. That's why you shouldn't feel bad about it."

Grant shrugged. He would have preferred having Horatio as a brother-in-law than anyone else, but if it wasn't meant to be, then it wasn't meant to be.

Carol entered the drawing room, and Lucinda jumped down from the settee to run over to her. Carol picked her up and gave her a hug. "Did you miss me?"

"Go outside," Lucinda replied.

Leave it to a child to be blunt. Grant rose to his feet and walked over to her and Lucinda. "Lucinda, that is rude. You need to welcome your mother home, tell her you missed her, and then ask if it's time to go out."

"Mama, missed you," Lucinda said.

She chuckled. "I missed you, too. And yes, we will go out soon. I notice we have a visitor." Her gaze went to Horatio who was standing up. "How are you today, Horatio?"

"I'm doing fine," he replied.

"Do you want to go to the circus with us?" Grant asked.

"I don't want to impose on your outing," Horatio said.

"I don't mind if you come along," Carol assured him when he glanced at her.

"Come with us," Grant encouraged. "You can't spend all your time thinking about investments."

"All right, I'll go," Horatio agreed. "Rachel says I spend too much time on my work. It'll be nice to do something fun."

"Ready to go, Papa?" Lucinda asked.

He picked her up and nodded. "Yes, we're finally ready."

The group made their way to the carriage out front, and Grant put Lucinda into the carriage after Horatio stepped into it.

Carol stopped him before he could help her in. "I want to give you something first," she said in a low voice.

Curious, he watched as she opened her reticle and pulled out a pink ribbon.

Despite the blush on her cheeks, she said, "I want to give you a token of my affection. Is this something you'd be willing to carry around with you?"

She held out the silky fabric to him, so he accepted it. He caught the faint hint of perfume on it. He sniffed it again. It was the scent he had come to associate with her. His heart warmed. This was the best gift anyone had ever given him. "I'd be honored to carry this with me. Thank you, Carol."

He could tell by the way her eyes lit up that his response pleased her. He would have kissed her if they were alone, but since they were in public, he settled for giving her hand an affectionate squeeze before helping her into the carriage.

<u>Coming Next in this series:</u>

Worth the Risk
(Book 4)

All of his life, Mr. Reuben St. George has been sickly. And his older brother has always done everything he could to keep him safe and healthy. So for all of Reuben's life, he's been forced to stay in the country. Then, finally, he's allowed to go to London to attend a Season with the hopes of finding a lady to marry. And he finds the perfect one for him. Miss Amelia Carnel.

Except London is a big place with a lot of people, and all it does is make him sick so often he is unable to attend quite a few social activities. The most frustrating part is that Amelia has other suitors. Healthy suitors who can give her lots of children who will also be healthy. As much as he hates to admit it, his brother is right. He needs to return to the country and let Amelia stay in London to marry someone who can give her the kind of life she deserves. It is with a heavy heart he leaves a farewell missive to the lady of his dreams.

But he never bothered to ask Amelia what she wants, and she's going to make certain he finds out. Some things are worth the risk, and love is one of them.

Other romances of interest:

If you would like to read Helena's romance…

Love Lessons With the Duke
(Marriage by Deceit Series: Book 2)

Camden Hollis, the Duke of Ashbourne, needs to pay off his brother's debts, but all he has is a troubled estate. So when he hears that Lady Seyton is known for teaching ladies what to do to secure marriages by the end of the Season, he comes to her for help.

Helena Walter, the Lady of Seyton, doesn't know what to think of Camden's unusual request. How could a titled gentleman who is so good-looking need help getting a wife? Her initial response is to turn him down, thinking he is merely wasting her time. But then she catches him bumbling through a conversation with a lady and realizes he–more than anyone–needs her help.

And so the lessons begin. But before long, Camden is convinced she's the perfect one for him. She, however, is a widow and is happy with her freedom. He might find it'll require a scandal to get the two things he wants most: a love match and securing his estate.

If you'd like to read Mr. Jasper's romance…

His Wicked Lady
(Marriage by Arrangement Series: Book 1)

Regan Alger, the Lady of Cantrell, is bored with her life. Yes, she's been more fortunate than most. She was once married to a wonderful gentleman, and this love resulted in her young son—a boy she loves more than anything. But even a son can't fill the void in her life. She misses having a husband, both in and out of bed, so when she happens to come across a gentleman at a ball who ignites her passion, she decides he'll be her next husband. And she's not the least bit shy about letting him know it.

Just as determined as Regan is to have Mr. Malcolm Jasper for a husband, he's equally determined to end up with anyone but her. If he marries her, his life will be one of chaos and scandal. He's sure of it. After all, she's much too outspoken and flirtatious. So he jumps at the chance for an arranged marriage, thinking once he secures a reputable and quiet bride, Regan will leave him alone. Little does he know, though, his sister and her two friends know Regan wants to marry him, and they are more than happy to help Regan get what she wants.

If you'd like to read Lord Steinbeck's romance…

The Earl's Wallflower Bride
(Marriage by Arrangement Series: Book 3)

Warren Beaufort, the Lord of Steinbeck, prides himself on having the best of the best. From his furnishings in his townhouse to his clothes, he chooses everything with the intention of impressing others. And more than that, he has amassed a fortune that is the envy of many in London.

One thing he lacks, however, is an heir. In order to get the heir, he'll need a wife. The lady must either come from significant money or she must be extremely beautiful. It matters little to him who he gets as long as he benefits somehow from the match.

Lady Iris, the Duke of Hartwell's daughter, has money, but she lacks both grace and looks. One thing she does have, however, is the good sense to know a gentleman like Warren is all wrong for her, which is why she's horrified to learn she's been matched with him for marriage. But the Duchess of Ashbourne and her friends assure her that she and Warren have so much in common they are an ideal match.

Having no way out of the marriage her father has arranged for her, she has no choice but to marry Warren. While she might have to give him the heir, she will never, under any circumstance, give him something far more precious…her heart.

All Books by Ruth Ann Nordin
(Chronological Order)

Regencies

<u>Marriage by Scandal Series</u>
The Earl's Inconvenient Wife
A Most Unsuitable Earl
His Reluctant Lady
The Earl's Scandalous Wife

<u>Marriage by Design Series</u>
Breaking the Rules
Nobody's Fool
A Deceptive Wager

<u>Standalone Regency</u>
Her Counterfeit Husband
(happens during A Most Unsuitable Earl)

<u>Marriage by Deceit Series</u>
The Earl's Secret Bargain
Love Lessons With the Duke
Ruined by the Earl
The Earl's Stolen Bride

<u>Marriage by Arrangement Series</u>
His Wicked Lady
Her Devilish Marquess
The Earl's Wallflower Bride

<u>Marriage by Bargain Series</u>
The Viscount's Runaway Bride
The Rake's Vow
Taming The Viscountess
If It Takes A Scandal

<u>Marriage by Fate Series</u>
The Reclusive Earl
Married In Haste
Make Believe Bride
The Perfect Duke
Kidnapping the Viscount

<u>Marriage by Fairytale Series</u>
The Marriage Contract
One Enchanted Evening
The Wedding Pact
Fairest of Them All
The Duke's Secluded Bride

<u>Marriage by Necessity Series</u>
A Perilous Marriage
The Cursed Earl
Heiress of Misfortune

<u>Marriage by Obligation Series</u>
Secret Admirer
Midnight Wedding
The Earl's Jilted Bride
Worth the Risk

Historical Western Romances

<u>Pioneer Series</u>
Wagon Trail Bride
The Marriage Agreement
Groom For Hire
Forced Into Marriage

<u>Nebraska Series</u>
Her Heart's Desire
A Bride for Tom
A Husband for Margaret
Eye of the Beholder
The Wrong Husband
Shotgun Groom
To Have and To Hold
Forever Yours
His Redeeming Bride
Isaac's Decision

<u>Misled Mail Order Brides Series</u>
The Bride Price
The Rejected Groom
The Perfect Wife
The Imperfect Husband

<u>Husbands for the Larson Sisters</u>
Nelly's Mail Order Husband
Perfectly Matched
Suitable for Marriage
Daisy's Prince Charming

Wyoming Series
The Outlaw's Bride
The Rancher's Bride
The Fugitive's Bride
The Loner's Bride

Chance at Love Series
The Convenient Mail Order Bride
The Mistaken Mail Order Bride
The Accidental Mail Order Bride
The Bargain Mail Order Bride

Nebraska Prairie Series
The Purchased Bride
The Bride's Choice
Interview for a Wife

South Dakota Series
Loving Eliza
Bid for a Bride
Bride of Second Chances

Montana Collection
Mitch's Win
Boaz's Wager
Patty's Gamble
Shane's Deal

Native American Romance Series
Restoring Hope
A Chance In Time
Brave Beginnings
Bound by Honor, Bound by Love

Thrillers

Return of the Aliens (Christian End-Times Novel)
Late One Night (flash fiction)
The Very True Legends of Ol' Man Wickleberry and his Demise
- Ink Slingers' Anthology

Fantasies

<u>Enchanted Galaxy Series</u>
A Royal Engagement
Royal Hearts
The Royal Pursuit
Royal Heiress

Nonfiction

<u>Writing Tips Series</u>
11 Tips for New Writers
The Emotionally Engaging Character
Writing for Passion
Making a Realistic Publishing Schedule

www.ingramcontent.com/pod-product-compliance
Lightning Source LLC
Chambersburg PA
CBHW070753160726
48004CB00001B/167